BOOK
OF
CLOUDS

BOOK
OF
CLOUDS

Chloe Aridjis

Black Cat
a paperback original imprint of Grove/Atlantic, Inc.
New York

Published simultaneously in Canada
Printed in the United States of America

FIRST EDITION

ISBN-10: 0-8021-7056-0
ISBN-13: 978-0-8021-7056-9

Black Cat
a paperback original imprint of Grove/Atlantic, Inc.
841 Broadway
New York, NY 10003

Distributed by Publishers Group West

www.groveatlantic.com

09 10 11 12   10 9 8 7 6 5 4 3 2 1

For my parents and Eva

BOOK
OF
CLOUDS

AUGUST 11, 1986
BERLIN

I saw Hitler at a time when the Reichstag was little more than a burnt, skeletal silhouette of its former self and the Brandenburg Gate obstructed passage rather than granted it. It was an evening when the moral remains of the city bobbed up to the surface and floated like driftwood before sinking back down to the seabed to further splinter and rot.

Berlin was the last stop on our European tour—we'd worked our way up from Spain, through France, Belgium and the Netherlands—and soon we would be flying home, back across the Atlantic, to start the new school year. My two brothers, still thrumming with energy, lamented that we had to leave. In every town and city they'd wandered off into the night and not returned until breakfast, answering in cranky monosyllables, between sips of coffee, whenever anyone commented on the amount of money being wasted on hotel rooms. My two sisters, on the other hand, weighed down by stories and souvenirs, were desperate to unload, and my parents too felt weary and ready for home. Not to mention that we'd used up 60 percent of the money we'd just inherited from my grandfather, and the remaining 40 had allegedly been set aside for our ever-expanding deli.

On our final evening, after an early dinner, our parents announced they were taking us to a demonstration against the Berlin Wall to protest twenty-five years of this "icon of the Cold War." Wherever you went in Berlin, sooner or later you would run into it, even on the day we visited Hansa Studios where Nick Cave and Depeche Mode used to record, or the secondhand shop that sold clothes by the kilo. No matter where you went—east, west, north, south—before long you hit against the intractable curtain of cement and were able to go no further. That was our impression, anyway, so we figured that we too might as well protest against this seemingly endless structure that limited even *our* movement, though we were just seven tourists visiting the city for the first time.

When we arrived at the demonstration there were already thousands of people gathered on the west side of the Brandenburg Gate, young couples, old couples, scampering children, punks with dogs, Goths, women with buzz cuts, men in blue overalls—a cross section, looking back, of what West Berlin had been in those days. Most people remained standing but there were also large groups spread out on the pavement, singing and chanting and passing around bottles of beer. Two nights before, we'd heard, a human chain had started to form along the Wall with an aim to cover all 155 kilometers.

On the east side, meanwhile, men in grey uniforms and steel helmets were marching up and down Karl-Marx-Allee. I envisioned dramatic clashes between metal and flesh, order and chaos, homogeny and diversity, but I knew that in real life these clashes were far more abstract. My parents had wanted to take us across the border to show us "a true portrait of Communism" but there had been a mysterious problem with our visas so we'd stayed in the West all week, left to imagine as best we could what life was like on the other side, ever more intrigued by notions of "this side" and "beyond."

People continued to arrive. The singing and chanting grew louder and I could hardly hear when anyone in my family leaned over to say something, as though on that night our language had been put on hold and German was the only means of communication. But there were other ways of having a voice, and before long we had joined the lengthy chain following the Wall and I found myself clasping the hand of a man with a ponytail and a black leather jacket until one of my brothers insisted on changing places with me. I tried to imagine the thousands of people across West Berlin to whom we would be connected through this gesture of solidarity but the thought was dizzying so I focused instead on the punks playing nearby with their dogs, as they threw what looked like battered tennis shoes, which the dogs would race to retrieve. The punks would then throw the bait in another direction, every now and then missing and hitting someone on the head or shoulder, the sight of which triggered boisterous rounds of laughter.

Twilight came on. Some of the organizers walked through the crowd passing out white candles. A number of people declined and flicked on their lighters instead. Against the sea of lights the Reichstag looked even gloomier and more

forsaken and the Brandenburg Gate, with its goddess of Vic-
tory and twelve Doric columns, doubly silenced by dusk. Not
far from us an old punk with a torch jumped onto the Wall
and screamed some words into the East, rabid words, though
we couldn't understand what he was saying. On the other side,
my mother told us, invisible eyes would be following his every
movement. There didn't seem to be anyone in the watchtowers across the way yet we imagined men in round caps with
cat slit eyes surveying the whole spectacle, ready to pounce
should any of us trespass one inch into their territory.

We stayed at the demonstration until the candles burned
down and the fuel in the lighters ran out and all the voices
grew hoarse, until our watches read midnight and people gathered their things and began to leave. We followed our parents
down the street, then down many more, in the direction that
everyone seemed to be heading. There was no chance of finding a taxi, we would have to take the U-Bahn, so along with
hordes of others we descended into Gleisdreieck station like
a screaming eight-hundred-headed monster.

The frenzied crowds made it impossible to get within
arm's reach of the ticket machines so when the next train
pulled into the station we jumped on without having paid. It
was one of those nights, we sensed, when anything was per-
mitted. Hundreds of people were crammed into the carriage,
it was impossible to even turn around, and with the heat my
sweater began to feel like a straightjacket but there was barely
enough room to remove it. After tugging on the zipper and

successfully extracting one arm I noticed that my family was standing at the opposite end of the car; swept up in the confusion, we must have boarded through different doors and now dozens of bodies were between us, though it didn't really matter since I knew where to get off, and as if in some bizarre Cubist composition, all I saw were corners and fragments of their angled faces, my mother's lips, my father's nose, my sister's hair, and I remember thinking to myself how this amalgam would have been far more attractive, a composite being, cobbled together from random parts of each, rather than the complex six-person package to which I was bound for life.

The train continued its journey and I began to examine the passengers sitting and standing nearby. There was general mirth in the carriage and I began to feel as if I was in some kind of aviary, though one populated with less exotic species than those we had at home. Groups of large black and grey birds with blond tufts laughed and told jokes while scruffy brown birds with ruffled feathers waved bottles of beer. Solemn birds read the evening paper, others squawked over crossword puzzles and the smallest birds, of which there were only a few, emitted the occasional chirp, as if aware of the hierarchy but uncertain how to participate. And then I noticed one bird, a bird with unusual plumage, which, unlike the others, didn't seem to want to draw attention to itself. Sitting directly in front of me was a very old woman, nearly a century old I would say, wearing a scarf that framed a wide forehead, which peered out like an angry planet. She had dark, deep-set eyes and a square, jowly face that was remarkably masculine. Stiff and erect, the old woman sat in her seat clutching her purse and stared straight ahead.

The jowly face, the sweeping forehead, the deep-set furnacy eyes, everything seemed horribly familiar and I felt as if I had seen this face before, but in black and white. Since I was standing directly in front of her I had the perfect perspective to really study it, and the more I stared the more certain I was . . . Yes, that it was Hitler, Hitler as an old woman, riding westwards. *This is Hitler,* I said to myself, *there is no doubt that this is Hitler.* The old woman had the same-shaped face, the same black eyes and high forehead, and, now that I looked again, even a shadowy square area where the mustache would have been. I stared and then I stared some more, petrified, horrified, amazed by what I saw. All of a sudden the train jerked around a curve. The woman, startled out of her rigid position and thrown back into the present, finally looked up and around and it was then that she caught me staring. I couldn't believe it: I was making eye contact with Hitler. Hitler was making eye contact with me. At least for a few seconds. The woman frowned and turned away, then back to me and smiled faintly, her lips barely moving, probably to ingratiate herself since my staring must have unnerved her.

My heart pounded. The sight in front of me, added to the stifling heat in the carriage, might have been enough to give anyone a heart attack, even me, at age fourteen, yet a heart attack at age fourteen was still more probable than seeing Hitler on the U-Bahn disguised as an old woman. How could it be, I wondered, that forty years after the war I found myself face-to-face with the devil himself, the devil whose very name cast a shadow on nearly every landscape of my young life? I waved to my brother Gabriel, who happened to glance my way, and made an urgent sign for him to join me even if he had to bulldoze his way through the crowd, but he took one glance at all the large Germans standing between us and shrugged. I then pointed at my parents, motioning to him to get their attention, but the fool just shrugged a second time and turned away. My mother, nose deep in a guidebook, was a lost cause, as was my father, busy trying to decipher the signs on the walls of the train. My two sisters were just as useless, huddled together in a conference of whispers, oblivious to everything but each other, and I couldn't even see my other brother, who was eclipsed by at least ten bodies.

My entire family stayed rooted like metal poles on the U-Bahn while I stood one foot away from Hitler with not a witness in sight. To my great surprise, *not a single person* seemed to notice the old woman in the head scarf. All these birds were simply too caught up in their feather ruffling and gregarious squawking to pay much attention to their fellow passengers, especially to those seated below eye level, on a different perch. But how could no one else notice the forehead and the eyes and the shaded patch between nose and mouth, when the combination of these features seemed so glaringly, so obscenely, real and factual and present?

We plowed deeper into the West. The train stopped at Wittenbergplatz and then, a few minutes later, at Zoologischer Garten. Dozens of people stepped out, freeing up the space considerably but my family stayed where they were. Now that the crowd had thinned, although there were still quite a few people between us, I noticed strapping men posted at each of the four doors of the carriage, four buzzards in their sixties or seventies, all wearing the same bulky grey coat. There was no need for these coats in August, coats cut from a cloth so thick it barely dented, and I couldn't help wondering whether they were hiding weapons beneath them.

Their eyes were riveted on the old lady. Every now and then one of them would turn to study the passengers around her, monitoring their movements with narrowed eyes, but most of the time they just watched her. *These are former SS men*, it then occurred to me, *here to guard the incognito hag, aging secret agents who survived the war and have for the past forty years lived in hiding with their Führer.* The old woman raised an arm to rearrange her scarf. Two guards tensed their shoulders, mistaking the gesture, fleetingly, for a command. I couldn't bear it any longer and again tried to wave my parents over, but my mother was glued to her guidebook, my father to the signs on the train, my sisters to their gossip and my brothers to who knows what.

At Sophie-Charlotte-Platz the old woman rose from her seat and brushed past me, her shoulder nudging mine a little harder than necessary. I moved aside. Within seconds all four men left their stations by the doors and closed in to form a tight circle around her. The train came to a halt. Two of the buzzards stepped out, then the old lady, followed by the other two. The grey gang had disembarked. The doors closed and the train, its load considerably lightened, continued on its way.

No one in my family believed me, not even my brother Gabriel, the most adventurous-minded of the lot. They told me it was absurd: Hitler shot himself in his bunker in 1945. It was common knowledge. His skull had been found by the Soviets and was on display in a museum in Moscow. There was more than enough proof. End of story.

Three years later, the Wall fell. And I, in one way or another, grew up.

The new neighborhood was happily free of references, banal or nostalgic, and the apartment satisfied all the usual criteria —fifteen minutes from a park, ten from a landmark, five from a bakery—and the rest was of little consequence. I would adjust. Since returning to Berlin in 2002 I had already lived in Charlottenburg, Kreuzberg and Mitte and now the time had come, perhaps belatedly given how fast things were changing, to try Prenzlauer Berg. After five years I still had the impulse, every ten to twelve months, to find a new home. Spaces became too familiar, too elastic, too accommodating. Boredom and exasperation would set in. And though of course nothing really changed from one roof to another, I liked to harbor the illusion that small variations occurred within, that with each move something was being renewed.

My latest dwelling was blessed with ceilings twice my height, wooden floors, double windows with brass knobs and an aluminum Soviet bathtub from the eighties that still had the factory label attached to the side. All in all, it was a good deal for three hundred euros a month and no doubt a step up from my last home on a sleepless junction in Kreuzberg. Like many old houses, this one had a front section, where I lived, and at the back an interior courtyard, the Hof, enclosed on all three sides by more apartments. Deprived of a street view, the main compensation for these homes at the rear was silence and little balconies. Some families seemed especially proud of their flower arrangements, miniature gardens jutting out of the concrete; for those not given to small-scale floriculture, this bonus section of suspended space was used to cram in any surplus object that didn't fit inside, from plastic tables to desk chairs to bicycles to laundry racks. I could look into these balconies from my kitchen window, which commanded a generous view of the Hof, although I preferred to focus on the old oak that rose in the middle, its thick trunk and changing leaves kindly blocking out the row of garish recycling bins behind.

On the afternoon of the storm, succumbing to the usual restlessness born of too much time between four walls, I slipped on a jacket and double locked the door. Out on the street a mild breeze stirred the smaller branches of the trees but left the larger ones at rest. It was late August and the air was warm, tending towards moist. As I stood outside my building deciding in which direction to walk I noticed a wrinkled face peering at me from behind the lace curtain of a ground-floor window. Two other faces, equally impassive, were stationed right behind. These were my neighbors from below, three ancient women, most likely widows from the war, and so far they were the only neighbors I'd seen. We had yet to exchange

a word but I felt certain that my arrival had furnished them
with material for discussion during their empty, loveless hours.

As for my own empty, loveless hours, how I spent them
varied from day to day, week to week. The money trickling in
from home helped supplement what little savings remained
from my last employment, as assistant to the assistant editor
of a second-rate psychology journal. After six months I no
longer wanted to know about the fickle tides of the human
brain, far too many to count, nor how to treat the pathologies
that rattle every one of us. As a matter of pride, I quit one day
before they were planning to annul my flimsy contract. I felt
dizzied by the odor of mothballs given off by Herr Schutz, my
employer, as he hovered over me while I cleared out my desk
drawers and erased all personal files from the computer. I
stuffed everything into an Aldi shopping bag while he hung
around in a cloud of camphor, checking that I wasn't taking
anything that wasn't mine.

On the corner outside my local bakery, one of those
places featuring long arrays of berry tarts, cream pies and cup-
cakes with radioactive pink icing, I watched four boys crowd
around a hatted woman as she opened a paper bag. Four pairs
of impatient hands clutched at the cinnamon buns that were
doled out, one by one. All of a sudden a gust of wind blew
the woman's hat off but the children failed to notice. Before
the woman could react, a passing deliveryman jumped off his
yellow bicycle and ran to fetch it. From inside the shop a
baker watched.

The day turned muggier, a column of hot, rising air encircling me as I went down the next street and then on to another and another. I paused outside the cracked windows of the once lively and now deserted Café Titanic, a mass of ivy obscuring half its sign. A few doors down the smell of varnish wafted out from the antiquarian's, where two polished mahogany tables, unsteady on their new bases, wobbled on the pavement.

The restless air was closing in and I decided to head back home. A plastic bag, the discarded ghost of the object it once carried, was blown toward me and clung to my leg for a few seconds before I managed to shake it off. Birds twittered nervously in the trees but were nowhere to be found, not a single beak, claw or feather when I looked up. And then they fell silent. The sky had grown a shade or two darker, a slate grey cumulonimbus blotting the horizon.

The atmosphere was changing fast, the air driven by a new buoyancy. The larger tree branches were swaying now too. Everything was in motion. Fiery strokes lit the sky, followed, a second or two later, by a low, steady rumbling. It was as if a herd of cattle, galvanized by the massive electrical sparks, had been set loose in the streets of Berlin. I quickened my pace.

Drops of rain began to fall. The drops became larger and more frequent. Before long, the streets turned into a vertigo of hurrying shapes. A squat woman, the top half of her body hidden under her umbrella, waddled by like a windup toadstool.

At the entrance to my building I noticed one of the old women at her window, looking for signs like the rest of us, but upon seeing me she quickly retreated behind the lace curtain. Back in my apartment I rushed through the rooms to close any windows that may have remained open—there were indeed two, in the kitchen and the bedroom—but not without difficulty. The mounting pressure fought to enter, a tremendous suction at each point of entry, as if the harbinger winds were seeking refuge from an advancing sovereign. I had to push hard. From the living room I could see treetops bending and awnings flapping, the breath of the storm. Everything was in motion.

Once I'd closed the windows there was nothing left to do but take a seat at the kitchen table and wait for the storm to pass. Seconds later the entire building swayed, just a centimeter I think, perhaps less, responding to the furious vacuum outside. I could feel it trying to suck us into its mobile chaos, into the powerhouse of energy churning within, enough energy to power a village for a year. The rain made a deafening sound, an uneven pour like the decanting of ten thousand aquariums, and I stood at my window, nothing but two panes of glass separating me from the torrent, watching as the rain washed the dirt from car windows, promises from fulfillment, a small bird from its nest.

Yet my building held tight through the wind and the rain and the thunder. Unable to uproot it, the storm finally marched off. It was a classic summer storm, a factory of hot weather. Our actual encounter was brief, a few minutes at most, and once the building finished swaying I walked through the rooms to see what might have changed. Everything was still in place, the objects on tables and shelves unmoved, even the glass of water by my bed showed no signs of having spilled over. The storm had not left anything in its wake, or so it seemed, until I noticed the dirt. Row upon row of dirt, risen from the cracks between the floorboards. Each room, apart from the bathroom with its seamless linoleum, was crossed by long caterpillars of dust. The dirt and dust of decades, I imagined, drawn to the surface by the sheer force of suction. It looked as if an army of termites had been unleashed. I spent twenty minutes sweeping it all up and another twenty wandering from room to room, with a growing hunch that although the storm had moved on, something in the building's very foundation had shifted, ever so slightly, revealing new fault lines.

The day after the storm the sky was empty, uninterrupted blue save for a white plume left by an airplane. When the kitchen clock struck two I decided to go for a walk to see what changes had been wrought. It was Sunday, the ideal day for strolling, even better than Saturday, and I needed to get out of the house.

Ever since arriving in Berlin I'd become a professional in lost time. It was impossible to account for all the hours. The hands on clocks and watches jumped ahead or lagged behind indiscriminately. The city ran on its own chronometric scale.

Days would draw to a close and I would ask myself what had been accomplished, how to distinguish today from yesterday and the day before. This was especially evident when I was between jobs. But no matter where I was in my life, I always preferred the anticipation of the weekend to the weekend itself. And there was also the fact, I couldn't deny it, that after five years in the city I had yet to find someone with whom to spend my Sundays. There had been the odd companion of a few weeks or months, like the dreamy but muddled student from the Humboldt or the raucous actor from the Volksbühne, never without his tweed cap, but nothing had ever lasted or even left a dent so with every Sunday sun arose the question of how to fill the hours. I had no problem spending Monday through Friday alone, Saturdays were neutral, but each Sunday had to be reckoned with. There's solitude and then there's loneliness. Monday through Saturday were marked by solitude but on Sundays that solitude hardened into something else. I didn't necessarily *want* to spend my Sundays with someone, but on those days I was simply reminded, in the nagging pitch that only Sundays can have, that I was alone.

The day after the storm was one of those Sundays. I put on a jacket and headed towards the Wasserturm, an old water tower surrounded by shops and restaurants. The air had cooled, the city had been stilled, everything was a few keys quieter. I passed Bar Gagarin on the corner and debated whether to go in. From what I remembered, the place served homemade borscht and thick slices of bread. As I stood deciding whether to enter or resume my walk, a black hairless dog appeared out of nowhere. He was a small dog, with dry, taut skin like that of a rhinoceros and a sparse black mohawk that ran from the top of his forehead down the nape of his neck. His tail was set low and tucked in, almost hidden from sight, his genitals as black as the rest of him.

Everyone noticed him at the same time and I watched in amusement as the Germans lunching outside laid down their knives and forks and stared in disbelief, unable, surely, to classify this creature with the shape and gait of a dog but lacking the other distinguishing feature, namely, fur. But I recognized him instantly, this Xoloitzcuintle, Xolo for short, member of the ancient canine breed from Mexico that in Aztec myth would guide human souls through Mictlan, the ninth and lowest circle of the labyrinthine underworld, to their eternal resting place. Only four thousand Xolos were said to exist but here was one, standing on a street corner in Berlin on a cool Sunday in August.

Oblivious, or simply indifferent, to the mural of inquisitive eyes, the dog singled me out and trotted over to where I stood. He lifted his head and gazed into my face. His own eyes were dark and shiny, emanating something unfathomable, almost prehistoric. I bent down to pet him, his skin strangely warm despite the chill in the air, and felt a dark mole on his cheek from which sprouted a tuft of coarse hairs. I asked the waitress for a bowl of water. The dog lapped it up in seconds, his tongue shockingly pink against the black of his body.

"Is that your dog?" the waitress asked.

I shook my head *no* while enormously tempted to nod *yes.*

"Well, who knows where he came from."

I knelt down and murmured some kind words into the Xolo's ear. Should I bring him home, I wondered, or take him for a walk? But what if his owner was at another café on the square? Yet he didn't seem to belong to anyone. I decided to circle the block and consider the options. I remembered once hearing that the skin of Xolos was especially susceptible to wind and sunshine and that prolonged exposure to the elements could lead to all kinds of cutaneous eruptions. Who looked after this dog in Berlin, and how did he endure the German winters? After centuries of warming souls in life and guiding them in death was this all he got in return? I would take him home.

But when I reached Gagarin eight minutes later, the dog was gone. A young couple kissing at a table stopped kissing to inform me that he had wandered off not long ago, in the direction of Kollwitzplatz. I did not know whether to believe them, they seemed quite distracted, but after not finding him anywhere near the Wasserturm I concluded that he had indeed left, and spent the rest of the afternoon searching every street and square in the vicinity. At one point I thought I saw him but it was only a shadow under a park bench. Once it grew dark I gave up and walked home, aware that he would be camouflaged by night. Over the next week I returned daily to Gagarin only to hear the waitress repeatedly confirm, with growing impatience, that no dog "of that sort" had been seen again. I left my number just in case.

After the summer storm the acoustic life of my building changed. From one day to the next, I began to hear new sounds, as if the removal of dirt deposits had freed up the gaps between floors, allowing every murmur from above to be heard below and vice versa. Coughs and sighs to creaks and thuds began to seep between the floorboards. They dropped in syllables onto my face, flustered the silence of my room. Often they would move away from the center and lap at all four corners and at the worst of times, when they were particularly loud, the overhead bulb would start to sway like a pendulum marking someone else's tempo.

The sounds only came at night. My sleeping patterns were upset. I couldn't sleep without silence and now this silence eluded me. What troubled me the most was that I could not imagine who was making these sounds—I had never seen anyone going up to the next floor and as far as I knew the second and third floors were uninhabited. The old ladies seemed firmly ensconced at ground level and I seldom ran into the young families living across the hall. From what I gathered, mail arrived for the ground floor and the first, for no one else. And yet there was no question that these sounds were coming from above, from the space directly over my bedroom.

As the days wore on my imaginings grew more elaborate. What if, I thought to myself as I lay in bed cursing, an old Goth lived in the apartment above, a Goth with jet black hair sizzled with grey, his lanky frame bent by a permanent hunch, a Goth with chipped teeth, ferrety eyes, pockmarked cheeks and two rows of silver skull rings that weighed down his fingers? The sounds I heard were of the Goth knocking on the floor, his crablike hands proposing an insomniac duel, a battle to determine which of us could best resist night, as if night were a household chore one could avoid or postpone.

For all I knew, the noises upstairs came from a nocturnal businessman who carried out deals with sleepless colleagues across the city, men with glow-in-the-dark attaché cases and flashlight pens, active campaigners for the "other" community. Whoever it was, I decided that someday, when I was feeling assertive, I would go up and complain. I should have moved to the forest long ago, I would think to myself, perhaps to the Black Forest although the place probably wasn't half as sequestered as I imagined, though no doubt there would be far fewer faces and voices, only the imperceptible cries of ants, the footsteps of spiders and the sound of trees growing. But the madness that remote places cultivate is not to be taken lightly and I've always found something particularly disquieting in madness left to quietly ferment on its own; the social functions required of us help us maintain, at the very least, an illusion of normality, and for that reason alone I had, until that point in my life, remained in the city.

*   *   *

There was yet another thing getting in the way of sleep. The summer storm hadn't only altered the acoustics in my building. I also noticed that since then the curtains in my room hung slightly differently, always too far to the right or too far to the left, and no matter how much I tried to rearrange them, cracks of light fought their way through. But the rod nailed to the wall, rather than the curtain itself, was to blame, for the rod was no longer straight and consequently skewed everything attached to it. There was therefore no way, especially during the day, of guaranteeing total darkness. At first this was not a problem since I had an aversion to naps and wore a sleeping mask at night, but after a while the sleeping mask began to feel like an albatross so I cast it aside.

Far worse than being nudged awake by sunlight each morning was being kept up by artificial light at night. All I longed for, apart from silence upstairs, was total darkness, but no matter what night of the week, no matter how late the hour, there was always a sliver of light shining in. I would turn away from the window, cover my face with an arm, lay a second pillow over my head, but it was impossible to escape. For a long time I had deplored the human fixation on light, or rather, on artificial light, even before learning the German word *Entzauberung* and agreeing with all those poets and philosophers who warned about modernity and technology intruding further and further upon the imagination. Well, I was now witness to a very serious sort of disenchantment, the disenchantment of night, when each day at around six or seven, depending on the season, dusk fell and the mania for lighting up the sky and denying darkness began. Night would never be mystical again, at least not in the city, and I sometimes had fantasies of flying through town and smashing every lit bulb, or at least those screwed into the impertinent lamps on my street, obliterating those bright and irksome reminders of the rest of humanity, if only for a few hours, before morning rose and everything revved back to life.

Sleeping patterns choppy and irregular, job search steady and even. I visited the nearest employment office on Storkower Straße and waded through their listings. I skimmed *Der Tagesspiegel* and *Berliner Zeitung* as well as a few smaller neighborhood publications. I wandered the streets and read postings in shop windows, momentarily considering everything from dog walker to assistant at a design-your-own-candle studio. On some days I felt attached to the city and assimilated, on others like some kind of botched transplant with a few renegade veins, but I had to carry on and the only way was to never stop looking. After five years my parents still sent a monthly money order for two hundred euros, not enough to pay the full rent but enough to cover half and help keep me afloat. These money orders, our only steady means of communication, were sent in envelopes addressed in my father's green ballpoint pen. As time went by the postcards and phone calls had slowed to a trickle and though we liked to blame Telmex, the Mexican telephone monopoly, there was no getting around the knowledge that the internet existed, as did discount calling cards and other means to cheaply bridge the distance between Berlin and Mexico D.F. We simply ignored them and laid the blame on Telmex each time that weeks, or even months, passed in silence, and often the only words from home arrived in four jagged lines of green: my name, whatever street I was living on, *Berlín, Alemania*.

Berlin, omphalos of evil, the place where World War II had ended and, according to some, where World War III would begin. I never imagined it would happen but here I was, in the country whose very right to exist had often been a subject of debate over dinner. We had visited once in the eighties, that was enough, but here I was again, already for half a decade.

At university I considered doing French but my teacher at the Institut Français killed the language for me by assigning Jacques Prévert for weeks on end and although my father kept insisting that not all French poets wrote like him I couldn't get Prévert out of my head each time I heard the words *pleurer* or *parole*, so after a customer at the deli left behind a Stefan Zweig novella in translation, I don't remember which, I decided to switch to German and enrolled at the Goethe Institute in the Colonia Roma. My teacher, Michael Roth, was a soft-spoken Bavarian with sunken eyes, while most of my classmates were dolled-up Mexican women engaged to German businessmen or else young trainees courted by those omnipresent conglomerates, ThyssenKrupp and Siemens. *Fahren, sagen, müssen, trinken, laufen, glauben, empfehlen*. Each of us had his or her own mission, personal or professional, but we were all fed the same set of stalwart verbs with which to tinker.

To everyone's amazement, and only slightly less to my own, I came in first in the Institute's nationwide exam. The prize: a year in Berlin, free room and board, advanced German classes and a citywide travel pass. After little deliberation I packed a suitcase and a carton of books. Only two of my siblings, Carlos and Yvonne, seemed to mourn my departure. The other two, Teresa and Gabriel, could scarcely hide their delight at seeing a slice of the competition go (everyone longed to become the next deli manager—after all, we ran the largest Jewish deli in the city), and their hugs at the airport were as limp as my mother's were suffocating.

And so it was that I joined one of the many migrations to Berlin, dealing with the highs and lows of my mid to late twenties in a city that sought out different fashions of its own, some sleek and many ungainly, sifting through piles of possibilities to find the right fit. As for my own past, I managed to shed a few layers while the city shed, or at least tried to shed, a few old garments too. At first I got lost in the shuffle and was far more familiar with the bars, clubs and other nightspots than with the wide avenues and their daytime denizens. Hangovers were frequent, especially cheap-wine headaches, and I smoked with such abandon that my lighters rarely lasted more than three weeks. Over time, however, night and day blurred into one and I began to spot club people prowling the bustling streets, eye-catching zombies with chipped nails and running mascara, popping in and out of cafes to refuel. I too learned to switch gears between German lessons and the city beyond, which seemed, on the whole, to speak a less meticulous language than that of our textbooks.

Once my grant from the Goethe Institute expired I embarked on a long string of jobs—I had no desire to return to Mexico just yet—ranging from the dire to the risible: the requisite stint as au pair, to a hyperactive boy who reminded me of Struwwelpeter; as Spanish tutor to the handful of students who could afford tutoring; at a copy center where the paper always jammed; stacking bread at a convivial health food shop, until the maggots took over; at the check-in at Glück auf Eis, an indoor skating rink; and as receptionist at an Austrian dentistry journal that boasted a readership of sixty-five. After the dentistry journal followed the second-rate psychology magazine whose readership wasn't much higher, and that's when my luck fizzled and for the first time ever there was no job lined up.

That is, until the old man with the need for a mechanical ear.

"No need to apply, just present yourself at ten thirty on Wednesday morning. Bring any references you may have," read the letter in trembling fountain pen. An old friend of my parents, a former neighbor who moved from Mexico to Berlin, was the link to Doktor Friedrich Weiss, a distinguished historian in his seventies with fourteen books to his name but no visible family or personal assistant. I didn't have much in the way of reference letters but assumed it wouldn't matter given the family connection.

*   *   *

In order to reach Savignyplatz, where the historian lived, I had to take the S-Bahn from Alexanderplatz, a seven-minute tram ride from my new home. Apart from the station itself with its grand steel arch and vintage red sign, I was inexplicably drawn to the 365-meter television tower, which, now that I was living back in the eastern part of the city, would serve as my beacon. Whenever I lost my way I'd need only search the sky for the massive metal sphere impaled on the tapering cement column and know that somewhere in its shadow lay my home.

As for the S-Bahn, it too was a wondrous thing, especially its elevated routes, and during each ride I'd fall into that limbo between origin and destination where thoughts are churned out in time with the wheels of the train but with far less purpose and linearity. It wasn't just the trancelike glide of the wheels, however, or the view out the window. It was the announcer's voice. I preferred this recorded voice to any other voice I had heard in my life, especially on days when I felt disconnected from the city, attached by the thinnest of strings.

"*Nächste Station: Friedrichstraße.*"

All it took were a few words to retighten the bond.

"*Ausstieg links,*" the announcer would add for those ignorant of which side to disembark.

There was a spring to his utterances, a buoyancy packed and delivered in anticipation of every stop, and I would put away my book or newspaper and sit back and listen to the stations as they were rolled off, one by one, uninterrupted—that is, if other presences didn't interfere, such as plainclothes ticket inspectors or junkie musicians, their pleas for attention like dark blood clots in the city's circulation.

That morning I was on my way to acquaint myself with another recorded voice, this one older and unscripted. After winding west for fifteen minutes, the S-Bahn dropped me off at Savignyplatz. The cobblestone streets and cross-cultural boutiques had always held a bit too much *charm* but as I searched for Doktor Weiss's address I was also reminded that the area had some of the finest bookstores in town, not just the large art bookstore under the S-Bahn arches but also the Autorenbuchhandlung on Carmerstraße and the Knesebeck Elf on Knesebeckstraße and one or two others I'd eyed several times without going in.

The historian buzzed me into the Hof, where I had the good fortune of almost immediately bumping into the cordial Hausmeister, who set down the ladder he was carrying to inform me that the person I sought lived on the ground floor of the first building to the right, a quiet, almost inconspicuous, building in speckled greys. "The door is open," he said, "but we just painted it so you might have to give it a good kick."

A good kick didn't prove necessary, only a good push, and once inside, past a wall of metal mailboxes, I found a door with

a brass plaque that read "Dr. F. W." It took two to three minutes before the person bearing those initials came to open it.

"You must be Tatiana."

"Yes."

"Come in."

Once he had probably been tall and slim but now a low
stoop lent a melancholic air to an otherwise somewhat impos-
ing demeanor. His lips were pale and chapped and slightly
pursed, nearly forming a pout, his eyes a sharp blue. Thin red
veins ran down his nose like tributaries branching off into an
invisible delta. The thick silvery hair, neatly brushed to the
side, did not shift an inch when he moved his head and I
thought I could detect a faint scent of gel or hairspray though
I wasn't certain, it could have been powder. The only unruly
features were his eyebrows, two thick, tangled arches of grey.
Everything else was sober and controlled.

I followed this figure, clothed in a dark blue robe that
trailed the floor, down a corridor with several closed doors and
into a sitting room with ancient chairs and sofas that looked
as if they hadn't been sat on in centuries. No dents or tears in
the upholstery, every tasseled cushion perfectly angled. On the
walls hung various landscape paintings, mostly low horizons
with menacing skies and tiny human figures dwarfed by their
surroundings.

He did not offer me a seat so we remained standing face-
to-face, and with his stoop we were almost exactly the same
height.

From our first encounter to the last, he would use the formal *Sie*.

"Can I offer you something to drink?"

"No, thank you."

"Not even a glass of water?"

"No, thank you."

"Fine then, let's discuss work."

He extracted a small, shiny dictaphone from a pocket in his robe. Beneath the robe, I now noticed, he wore black pants and a grey woolen turtleneck.

"I have spoken hours and hours into this machine," he said, waving it before my eyes. "Hours and hours. Of thoughts and information. It needs to be transcribed. And I'm no good at typing."

I nodded.

"Is your German perfect, fluent enough to catch everything I say?"

"I think so."

"How long have you been in Berlin?"

"Over five years."

"And you studied German before coming?"

I nodded again. My answers seemed to satisfy him.

"Three days a week. Monday, Wednesday, Friday. Eleven to three. Does that work for you?"

"Yes."

"Fifteen euros the hour. Does that work for you?"

"Yes."

"And are you a good speller?"

"I think so," I answered, though far from certain.

"Very good. Now, please follow me."

He opened a door across the corridor and showed me into a room containing a wooden table with two drawers, a swivel chair and two filing cabinets. Long shelves lined each wall, each shelf sagging under the weight of hundreds of journals and old editions of *Encyclopaedia Britannica* with fractured leather spines. On the table a computer was humming away, an old desktop model that probably wouldn't have fetched more than a hundred euros, beside a halogen lamp and a mug with the image of the Berlin bear holding an assortment of pens and pencils.

Doktor Weiss handed me the dictaphone.

"I assume you know how to use these things?"

"It's just like a tape recorder, isn't it?"

"Yes. *Play, Pause, Rewind.* All of that. Do you feel ready or would you rather start tomorrow?"

"I can start now."

"Very good," he said, and smiled for the first time, a measured smile with closed lips. "There's a new file open on the computer. Just begin typing. I'm in the room across the hall should you have any questions. Please knock first."

Without another word Doktor Weiss shuffled out, in shoes I had yet to see since they were hidden by the robe, and closed the door behind him. I sat down at the computer, ran my fingers across the keyboard like a pianist warming up, and pressed *Play* on the dictaphone, which was very light.

The first text Weiss gave me to transcribe mapped out his ideas for a collection of essays he was planning to write, most of them to do with the phenomenology of space, specifically in Berlin. Spaces cling to their pasts, he said, and sometimes the present finds a way of accommodating this past and sometimes it doesn't. At best, a peaceful coexistence is struck up between temporal planes but most of the time it is a constant struggle for dominion. Objects would also form part of the inquiry, Weiss added, the reverberation of objects, the resonance of things long banished or displaced. If moved from their original position would they still resonate and if so, at the same level or in another key or octave?

As for the historian's voice, it was mesmeric, not quite as mesmeric as that of the S-Bahn announcer but as close as any other voice would ever come. More than anything, it had to do with the timbre and serenity with which he delivered his words. Weiss must have had pretty strong lungs, the lungs of a stage actor or radio presenter or someone required to ramble on for minutes on end without a break, for he never seemed to run out of breath, even during sentences that took up an entire page. I imagined that he spoke into the dictaphone while sitting in an armchair in a study filled with books, although sometimes I pictured him pacing back and forth along the corridor, going on conversational strolls with his metal rectangle.

Each word was uttered as distinctly as possible and the few times I had doubts I had only to consult the fortress of information that surrounded me, though I quickly realized that most of the journals dated back to the seventies and eighties and that the volumes of *Encyclopaedia Britannica* too were severely outdated.

On my first day at work I found myself staring at the blank screen as I listened to the sentences emerging from the dictaphone and didn't stop to write until ten minutes had gone by and I realized I hadn't transcribed a word. It seemed a shame, almost sacrilege, to interrupt the flow and replace the oral richness with mute text. Over the first month this happened often, and my transcriptions therefore took longer. The whole side of a tape would reach the end and I would have to go back and listen to it all over again, this time with my fingers poised on the computer keys. Weiss's sentences tended to run on and on, and I had to constantly press *Stop* and *Rewind* in order to catch the last few things he had said. After a few sessions, however, my typing grew faster and my hearing more attuned to his voice, and I was able to take in many long, winding passages without having to pause.

Confronted with incomplete sentences and pages of words with no break, I began taking the liberty of starting new paragraphs where I saw fit. I wasn't sure whether the historian wanted his stream of words reproduced as the same interrupted flow on the page or whether he'd welcome these minor editorial interventions, but I couldn't resist. He never commented on anything so I continued doing this up until the final transcription.

Before long I became more acquainted with Doktor Weiss's recorded voice than with his live one, which was a few notes higher and notably more weakened by age. In real life his voice occasionally cracked, and he seemed to prefer short sentences that trailed off at the end, leaving thoughts unfinished though I could usually guess what he intended to say.

I don't think he expected much eloquence from me either. Our silent relationship suited us both and for a long time neither of us made any attempts at widening the scope of our interaction. Niceties were ignored and etiquette, except the most basic, was left at the door, as if deemed too trivial to enter the house. I would ring the bell at eleven sharp, or sometimes at five past, and he would answer after two rings, always letting me wait for a few minutes, always in his dark blue robe that swept the floor, always with a quick nod hello. Occasionally he would murmur *Good morning* or even *How are you?* but he didn't await a response and I was pretty certain he didn't care whether my morning was good or whether I was fine, as long as I carried out the job. I would nonetheless reply politely and walk straight to my room at the end of the corridor, sit down and transcribe until three. He spoke, I typed. History without pens.

When it was time to leave I would usually find him standing outside the room, and when he wasn't there I would knock on the door of his study, often more than once, at first lightly and then a little harder. At the entrance we would bid our good-byes, Weiss always looking past me rather than into my eyes, and I would hear his door close as I walked past the row of mailboxes in the corridor, feeling, as the days wore on and I transcribed more and more words, that this minimum level of interaction must, at some point, give way. And yet I never attributed his behavior to any deliberate coolness or hostility but rather to a reserve, all too familiar, bred by many unpeopled hours.

Another Sunday had arrived, one more notch in the unrelenting parade of Sundays, bringing with it the prospect of a walk. Rather than set out aimlessly, I headed towards Boxhagener Platz, the site of an animated flea market I hadn't been to in months. It would be good to circulate in a crowd, I figured, prodded on by strangers too caught up in the visual onslaught to pay much attention to anyone in their midst.

The market was especially busy that afternoon. Long banks of furniture, outlandish clothes, a hodgepodge of crockery, vintage records: all was up for grabs, prices arbitrary (two euros for a skirt, twenty for a shabby belt) but negotiable. At the end of one row of stands sat a gaunt Russian, his face a familiar blend of boredom and melancholy, the ironed-on image of a Russian rock band fading from his T-shirt. Beneath his beige cap his nose stuck out like the muzzle of a malnourished fox. A thick, ruddy-cheeked woman stood near him, cigarette in one hand, baby carriage handle in the other. Like someone in a trance she pushed the carriage back and forth, back and forth, back and forth, but the baby inside, if indeed there was one, never made a squeak and all I saw when I peered in was a heap of blankets. Fanned out on the table before them lay an assortment of sad objects: a doorless birdcage, stuffed animals with missing eyes, a knapsack with a broken zipper, porcelain cups so thin they'd crumble between the lips.

After surveying a few other stands, mountains of junk with the odd gem thrown in, and getting shoved a little too often by zealous bargain hunters, I decided I'd had my fill for the day. On my way towards one of the exits I passed the Russians again. From the looks of it, sales were slow. The man was resting his hand on a fist and the woman continued to rock the baby carriage. With her free hand she offered her companion a cigarette, which he smoked down in long, deep drags, and when it was no more than a glowing stub he threw it to the ground and pounded it with a worn boot, then dropped his head to check that it had been extinguished, bones jutting from his nape like a small mountain ridge.

Just as I prepared to leave, aware that it was only a matter of time before my indiscreet staring would be noticed, I spotted an item on the table that looked less dilapidated than the rest.

"That is sound machine," the woman said as soon as I picked up the plastic contraption shaped like a seashell. Beneath its lid glistened two rows of labeled square green buttons.

"Good working," she added. "Thirty euros."

The man's gaze remained fixed on a group of noisy Spanish tourists in sunglasses.

"Can it be turned on loud, very loud?" I asked.

"Loud, yes," the woman confirmed.

I handed over a ten and a twenty, the last money of the week, and watched as the woman wrapped my apparatus in a torn supermarket bag.

Upon returning home I found, slipped under my door, a document containing a new clause the landlords had decided to add to the contract, stipulating in fine print—and in Germany fine print was taken to a whole new level though the irony of the term was often lost—that all tenants in the building must, four times a day, open each and every window for fifteen minutes in order to let fresh air into the apartment. Four times a day. Fifteen minutes at a time. That seemed like quite a commitment. But I decided to try it out. The next morning before going to work I walked through every room and opened the windows wide, then sat down and timed it. Fifteen minutes later, I got up and pulled them all closed. Five or six hours later, after returning from Weiss's, I went through all the rooms once more and opened the windows though the air inside still felt fresh. I waited fifteen minutes, then closed them. I ate some reheated pasta and went for a walk, stopping at the bakery for a whole-grain baguette, and when I got home I again opened all the windows for fifteen minutes. By the fourth fresh air session, following dinner, I lost track of time and forgot to close them until a chilly draft reminded me to do so.

After this experiment I opened and closed my windows only when I saw fit, rarely more than once a day and certainly for longer than fifteen minutes at a time, wondering whether someday a surveyor would appear, armed with a special gadget for measuring the level of stale air in the apartment, and fine me for not having cooperated with the national obsession with airing out, for not having opened the windows to let out the stale air and whatever else needed *airing out* in the apartment.

The air in Doktor Weiss's apartment did not seem to circulate much either, at least not in the room where I worked. The one window was kept bolted shut—a square of blue, white or insipid grey depending on the weather—and I would sit with the door closed since my desk faced the wall and for as long as I can remember I have hated the sensation of people approaching me, unannounced, from behind.

Not that I had to worry. Weiss himself spent the day behind the closed door of his study and so far he had entered my room on only two occasions: once to see whether he had perhaps left his box of paper clips on my desk and the second time to consult a journal from one of the shelves. He never lowered his eyes to see what was on my computer screen, nor did he inquire how far along I was in the transcriptions. At the end of each workday, at ten to three, I would print out the new pages (a rudimentary printer had one day appeared beside the computer) and leave them lying out. By the time I returned, two days later, the pages had always been removed.

* * *

"Where did you grow up?" Weiss asked one afternoon as we walked towards the door, the historian leading the way in his long blue robe that seemed ever more attached to his body, like a tree wrapped in years of ivy.

"Mexico City," I replied.

"Of course," he answered. "That is how you came to me. Your former neighbor."

"My parents' former neighbor."

"I was once there, in Mexico City, many years ago. 1967. I had a good friend, a photographer from Budapest named Chiki Weisz. Ever come across him?"

"No."

"He was married to Leonora Carrington."

"I don't know them."

By the time we reached the front door the historian's face had regained its usual solemnity. I don't know whether he was unimpressed that I didn't know his friends, or whether he felt we'd spoken quite enough and it was now time to reseal the gap, or whether, simply, we had reached the door and there was nothing more to say.

I had yet to see the kitchen or any other room of the apartment; all I knew was the entrance, the long corridor, the sitting room we briefly stepped into on my first day, and my room with its desk, sagging shelves and two filing cabinets. Of course Weiss showed me the bathroom too, a damp, tiny space hung with framed photographs of the historian as a young and surprisingly dashing man. Some pictures were

studio shots with excessive backlighting, others showed him
in a black cap and gown receiving his university diploma or
at a podium addressing packed theaters, yet others had him
posing beside the likes of Isaiah Berlin or Teddy Kollek, the
former mayor of Jerusalem.

And yet the telephone never rang, nor the doorbell. No
one came to seek out this elderly historian although his rank
in modern scholarship was, as far as I could tell, undisputed,
at least judging by the journals on the shelves around my desk.
Nearly every publication I opened contained an article by him
and the few issues that didn't had references to his work and,
often, long quotes. I had yet to find a Berlin-themed bibliog-
raphy that didn't list the name Friedrich Weiss beside the titles
of his most revered books: *Berlin: The Wounded City; Walter
Benjamin & Joseph Roth, Berlin Chroniclers Between Wars;
Musings from Both Sides of the Iron Curtain.* In retrospect, no
book or publication dated from beyond the eighties, but I
didn't think much of it at the time and besides, it was always
possible that he kept more recent periodicals in his study and
that my room was used to store less current material.

Apart from a distant yapping I heard one afternoon,
Weiss's home was free of foreign sounds, blissfully removed
from the clatter of neighbors, and the only thing I would hear
as I sat at my desk was my own tapping of computer keys and
pressing of dictaphone buttons. Every so often I would hear
the historian cough or clear his throat or the opening and clos-

ing of a door, but these sounds did not disturb me, especially since they came so rarely.

There were no indications that Doktor Weiss had any kind of social life and the only hint of a visitor was a half-used lipstick I once found lying on the bathroom sink beside the Heno de Pravia soap. Burnt sienna. Perhaps Weiss had a lady friend who visited in the evenings. Yet it seemed un-likely. His books, articles and murmured notes were all open for inspection but as for the man himself, as they said, *Er ließ sich nicht lesen.*

On my way home from Weiss's one afternoon, I came face-to-face with one of my neighbors. I'd contemplated slowing down as it became clear that we would reach the entrance at the exact same time and be forced into a greeting. But there seemed little point; she had already seen me and we were only a few feet apart and sooner or later, anyhow, we would run into each other, so perhaps it was best to get things over with once and for all.

With her torso tilting forwards and two short arms dangling in front, she looked strikingly like a *Tyrannosaurus rex*, a *T. rex* with wispy white hair, a beige raincoat and two Kaiser's shopping bags. I had seen her before, of course, but behind a distant, hazy window. She was one of the old ladies from below.

We reached the door, as expected, at the same time, and each began fishing for our keys, she in her cream-colored purse and I in my black canvas bag.

"And you are . . . ?" Her voice sounded creaky, as if out of use.

"Ta . . ."

The woman cocked her head. I fumbled with the strap of my bag and pulled out a few loose threads.

"Ta . . ." I began again, but couldn't bring myself to finish.

By now she had found her keys but instead of opening the door she just stood there, clutching them in her freckled hand while two drilling eyes surveyed me from head to toe, searching for clues, indicators to expand on, little hooks on which to hang her stories.

"Yes?"

"Ta . . ."

Until my name was spoken, I knew, there was no chance of getting past.

"Ta . . . tia . . . na."

"Tatiana?"

I nodded.

"Well, have you noticed, Tatiana, that since that dreadful storm (*schrecklich*, she said) the front door no longer closes properly, that anyone from the street can enter our building?"

"No, I hadn't."

"It's been weeks now. We've called the Hausmeister but he hasn't come. So make sure you pull it well closed each time."

"Okay."

"By the way, I'm Frau Heller."

After these words, issued so matter-of-factly, she pushed the door open without inserting her key in order to illustrate the problem. Why she'd searched for her keys in the first place was a mystery.

I managed to catch the door before it swung shut, wishing I could retract my name, which I now felt I'd offered too freely, and what did I care whether her name was Heller or

Müller or Surminski or Schmidt, I hadn't asked in the first place; for me they would always be, quite simply, *the three old ladies from below.*

As for my other neighbors, I rarely saw any of them, although twice a day I would hear their movements: the nimble footsteps of children, the plodding shuffle of fathers, the gentle tread of mothers. Life's tempo, quickening at dusk and dawn.

Sometimes I would feel the eyes of the Hof upon me, especially when the time came to take out the garbage and out of nowhere a head would emerge from one of the balconies and bring my attention to the green recycling bins reserved for glass or the yellow bins reserved for plastic or the blue-lidded bins reserved for newspaper and cartons. I knew where everything went but the community in the Hof liked to have a say in things and there was always someone on the alert, no matter the hour, whenever I entered our communal area with its thousand eyes.

Meanwhile, the sounds upstairs continued. And as became apparent once I left Mexico, sounds are always louder when you are on your own. Growing up, nocturnal sounds had never been a problem. I shared a bedroom with my two sisters while our brothers slept next door. Silence was hard to come by, secrets even more so. There was nothing to hide, nowhere to hide it. Strangely, I couldn't remember any particular sound from those years.

One night at around eleven, it may have been later, my upstairs neighbor began to move around more noisily than usual. I wasn't sure whether I was hearing thuds or giant footsteps, but it sounded like he or she was rearranging the furniture, trying out different configurations without settling on a single one. Each loud thud produced a vibration, not even earplugs would work. It was time to bring out the sound machine.

I read through the list of sounds on offer: small waves, tall waves, plunging waterfalls, rain (ranging from drizzle to thunderstorm), wind blowing through a variety of landscapes (fields, forests, cities), birds chirping, woodpeckers drilling, pigeons cooing, rainforest noises, desert noises, jungle noises. Each sound could be pitched higher or lower and mixed with others (for instance, one could have pigeons cooing in the middle of a windy desert). Deciding on small waves complemented by birds chirping softly, I turned off the light and closed my eyes. The waves commenced, the chirping began. Before long I could no longer hear my neighbor. But with each chirp my agitation grew. I imagined the raw pink gullets of young birds with open beaks whose parents had left the nest to seek food, encountered danger in some distant quarter and never returned. The chicks would wait and wait, their chirps increasingly frantic, until they rolled out of their nests and crashed to the ground or starved to death in the abandoned nest. I cancelled the birds and kept the waves. But the waves, the sound of the waves triggered images of helpless creatures at the mercy of the tide, of roaming ghost ships that know no shore, of a salty blackness that strangles.

The light back on, I weighed my other options. Pigeon cooing could work, since it reminded me of the city, a far safer place than the countryside. There are few things more irksome than the stillness of a country night, far from the hum and crackle of modernity. The unbroken darkness would of course be welcome but not the thought of being the only soul awake for miles nor, as stated earlier, of handing oneself over to the psychosis that remote places inspire. Lights off again, pigeons at low volume. My thoughts started to untangle, a sure sign that sleep was near, and I recalled a scruffy pigeon I'd seen years ago at an outdoor café in Mitte. My friend and I were having a beer when the bedraggled bird landed on our table, then bounced clumsily to the ground by our feet. He was clearly a grandfather pigeon, old age and ugliness excluding him from the community, left to fend for himself while the younger generations established their authority over the city squares. A few other pigeons were strutting about, but only the scruffy one drew near. His feathers were soiled and patches of crusty skin dotted his neck; his head was nearly bald and one of his eyes was scrunched closed.

Circling our table, the pigeon swiveled his head from side to side and pecked at the empty ground. Most of his right foot was missing, reduced to a calloused pink stub on which he hobbled. My friend pointed out that most urban pigeons suffered such a fate in their lifetimes. Cities were full, he said, of traps and wires and things that catch. Upon hearing this I hailed our waiter and ordered a basket of bread. The pigeon cocked its head with renewed interest. But by the time the bread arrived, minutes later, it had flown off, a dirty rag ascending into the sky.

I scrapped the pigeon sounds and opted for the waterfall, a safer bet since I'd never seen a proper, full force waterfall, only tame, artificial ones in public parks or in photographs of private gardens belonging to Latin American presidents. As the program resumed I settled into my pillow, imagining the water plunging and crashing onto the rocks below, plunging and crashing, plunging and crashing. The next morning, the machine was still turning out the sound of that angry surge tumbling through imaginary space.

When I returned to Boxhagener Platz the following Sunday, the sound machine wrapped in the torn bag in which it was purchased, the Russians were gone. Their stand had been replaced by an enterprise selling presumably flashier items of East German *Ostalgie*: a whole tea set, white porcelain with green borders, on whose cups the words "Made in G.D.R." were stamped in blue capitals; a poster illustrating various fonts, testimony to East Germany's enduring commitment to typographic excellence; old remote controls for defunct machines; industrial-size waffle irons. Each object a veritable collector's item, the young women at the stall assured me.

Some passages were wistful and poetic, others more factual and restrained, and in general I preferred the wistful and poetic, provided Weiss didn't get too carried away, which was seldom the case. One of the most recent transcriptions had been about forgotten street corners. Citing Walter Benjamin's *Berlin Childhood circa 1900*, he spoke about certain corners in Mitte and Charlottenburg, corners that once held sway over a child's imagination, but were later reduced to grey cement angles devoid of meaning. Weiss spoke, in that unwavering tone of his, about childhoods that remained childhoods forever, never to have known other stages of life, and about revered teachers, figures of unimpeachable authority who could do no wrong in a child's eyes, demoted in status from god to dog. And about cabinets and wardrobes and other hermetic items of furniture, repositories of magical secrets (especially when closed) that were carted off, hacked to bits and torched, their imagined contents vaporized without witnesses. And about satchels of illustrated books, a last hurrah for the imagination before the cast-iron lid was thrown on and everything, from one moment to the next, was extinguished. Destroyed allegories of the past, he called them, whole inventories of wonder voided of meaning.

Shortly after the Benjamin passage came another "text" pertaining to childhood, this one about drawings done by East Berlin children during the Cold War. Most of the illustrations, now stored at a city archive, had been done with colored pencils or crayons, a few were watercolors and two looked like the work of a blue ballpoint pen. The material varied, as did the style and degree of talent, but they all seemed to express one thing: a longing for freedom. Attempts to grasp the situation. Imaginings of what lay on the other side. One girl had drawn a turtledove flying over the Wall, on its way to visit its grandmother who lived in a nest deep in the foliage of a tree on the Kurfürstendamm. Another child offered nothing but a large, empty square: the view from his first floor apartment, which looked onto a section of dead, concrete Wall. Another schoolboy, a dexterous six-year-old, drew a family of ants armed with baskets of food and winter hats, crawling under the 155-kilometer-long construction. Other children had drawn houses without doors or houses with doors but no doorknobs, or watchtowers that reached high into the sky, higher and higher and higher, until they touched the moon.

I'd just finished the passage when Weiss knocked and entered the room, so silently he seemed to be floating.

"I was wondering whether you were free tomorrow afternoon?" he asked as he approached my desk, halting a foot away.

"I am."

"Good. I'd like you to carry out some fieldwork for me. A brief interview. If it goes well I will ask you to do others."

I nodded, eager to hear more.

"These short interviews will complement some of the passages you transcribe. It's important to keep the material up-to-date."

"Will you provide the questions?"

"Of course. Tomorrow, if indeed you are free, I will send you to interview one of these children. The boy who drew the ants. He lives rather east, from what I gather. Does six o'clock suit you?"

"Yes."

"Good. I will call him now to confirm. It goes without saying that you will be paid the extra hour or two."

Since I'd finished transcribing for the day I leafed through one of the M volumes of *Encyclopaedia Britannica*, skimming articles from the *MER* section at random while waiting for Weiss to return with the necessary details. My eyes jumped from page to page, taking in few of the words or illustrations, more alert to the smell and rustle of old paper, and after a few minutes I began to fret about my ability to conduct an interview. I'd never interviewed anyone in my life, much less in German, but then again, how hard could it be, especially if the questions were already written? The entries under *MER* held no answers, and, without ingesting more than a few ounces of unrelated information, I read about the cartographer Gerardus Mercator and the historian Louis-Sébastien Mercier and the Roman Catholic congregation the Sisters of Mercy (until then, the name of a rock band to me) and the Russian poet and essayist Dimitri Sergeyevich Merezhkovsky. I was nearing the end of the *MER*'s, starting to wonder when, if ever, someone had last turned these pages, when Weiss knocked and entered with the address.

His name was Jonas Krantz. He was thirty-six years old and therefore nineteen when the Wall came down. The ant drawing dated from the midseventies, and he was apparently the only child Weiss had contacted who still remembered having drawn what he had. During the eighties, Weiss told me, his parents had hidden the drawing in a phone book for fear that an informer would interpret the piece as a children's illustration of a plan he'd heard being hatched at the dinner table. He was now, the historian added with a chuckle, an accredited meteorologist.

Jonas Krantz lived in Marzahn, a proletariat area of Berlin I had yet to set foot in, and though most of it wasn't featured on the city map I'd carried around in my pocket since the day I arrived, I knew it lay beyond Prenzlauer Berg and Friedrichshain and, depending on where you were coming from, beyond Lichtenberg, more terra incognita. Somewhere there was a village, the village of Alt-Marzahn I'd heard, but Krantz apparently lived in the newer part.

I emerged from the Ring S-Bahn and entered the land of the Plattenbaus, which seemed even more looming and vast than those in Alexanderplatz and its immediate vicinity. Here the prefabricated concrete edifices overwhelmed the horizon, which was otherwise quite low, and had been repainted in playful colors with Rubik's cube patterns, alternating red and blue squares, or else in soft pastels, the lower half pink and the top half baby blue; yet others were bright red with green windows and balconies, but they all resembled huge Lego blocks, a delirium of squares or dice cast onto a flat, monotone terrain.

I turned off the main avenue, Landsberger Allee, and onto a curving street that branched off into different Plattenbau "communities" where, as far as I could tell, the mantra of Communist housing still felt very present in the layout. Each lot had three massive buildings enclosing a square equipped with a playground and a small communal space full of trees. Some even had a school and supermarket or miniature shopping center, creating the impression that each area was self-ruling or self-sufficient, as if it had its own central nervous system and all you had to do was touch one nerve and every inch of the place would reverberate. I saw only one guy with a cocky strut but otherwise the people I passed simply looked like working-class folk getting on with their day, lots of women of different ages walking their dogs, young Vietnamese smoking cigarettes at the entrances to supermarkets, a group of elderly Russians gathered around a park bench. Dusk was falling but the silvery light suited the place, which seemed both frozen in time and strangely futuristic.

A strong gust of wind blew up from behind like a prankster child and I stopped at a corner to button my coat. Just as I was slipping the final button into its hole I caught sight of a poster hanging from a streetlamp a foot or so above eye level, propaganda for the parliamentary elections that were coming up. I hadn't been following closely but you would have had to be blind not to notice the sea of paper plastered across the city in those days. From afar the image looked like an upright rectangle but from up close I saw it was a photo of a tombstone or some kind of memorial bearing Hebrew script, presumably from one of the Jewish cemeteries I had yet to visit. Below the tombstone, covered by bright green moss, ran the words, "WE'LL LET THE GRASS GROW OVER." The three capital letters glaring out from the lower left-hand corner confirmed my suspicion that this poster belonged to the NPD, which when I first moved to Berlin I interpreted as Narcissistic Personality Disorder before learning, pretty quickly, that it stood for a much uglier strain of self-love, the *Nationaldemokratische Partei Deutschlands*, Germany's right-wing extremist party. I quickened my pace, crossing a playground where kids whizzed back and forth on metal swings and two teenagers furtively traded the contents of their pockets, searching for a house number in a row of colorful Plattenbaus, three overgrown triplets unpacked from their industrial womb.

"*Hallo?*" A young male voice answered after I'd finally found the building on Allee der Kosmonauten and then the buzzer, one among one hundred, the names stacked gridlike, a tiny Plattenbau in itself, and rang eight times in a small fit of panic.

"This is Tatiana. I've come to conduct an interview for Doktor Weiss."

"Come in. Eighteenth floor."

The inside of the building was cold and sterile, its cheerless tiles and antiseptic smell reminding me of an enormous bathroom or a hospital. I shared the elevator up with a dour man in his forties who did not take his eyes off me. He ground his teeth loudly and I felt that at any moment he would snap, like a patient prescribed the wrong medication and just waiting for someone to blame.

My shoulders untensed once we reached the eighteenth floor.

"*Hallo!*" a voice called out from down the corridor.

I'm not sure what I was expecting. The name Jonas Krantz conjured up vague images of someone small and jovial, perhaps even a little gnomelike, but I was somewhat taken aback to see that the six-year-old draughtsman had ripened into a robust adult with a broad chest and coarse features. He had a blunt nose, probably broken once or twice, and a mouth that didn't close completely, with a small crack between the lips that made it seem as if they were on permanent standby, ready to eat or kiss or answer a question. Half his face lay in shadow; he hadn't shaved in days.

Yet the roughness of his appearance was offset by two things: a very gentle manner, I soon discovered, and by raccoon-ringed eyes born, I assumed, of chronic insomnia. It had always mystified me, this secret connection between eyelids and eye bags, the silent dominion of the shutter over the semicircle, I thought to myself as Jonas Krantz held out a large hand and introduced himself.

"Did you have trouble finding the place?"

"Yes. Everything looks the same."

"Only at first," he said, leading me into a sparsely furnished living room—a table, four chairs and a carved wooden bench—where he offered me a chair with missing rungs. Before sitting down I glanced over at the table, drawn to the intriguing collection of diagrams, sundials and glass tubes spread out on the surface. Amidst the instruments lay an empty bottle of Beck's and a metal ashtray overflowing with white and yellow stubs.

The table wasn't the only thing that caught my attention: on the walls of the room hung tan-and-green weather maps, charts showing, I imagined, past, present and future meteorological conditions, with red tacks protruding from the particularly nebulous areas, as well as huge maps of the oceans and continents with groups of straight and curved arrows pointing in different directions, presumably indicating some kind of flow.

"My home doubles as my weather station," Jonas said, taking a seat in a chair facing mine, this one with rungs. "From here I can read and record most things happening in the sky."

"I imagine you can see a lot from the eighteenth floor."

"Yes, and I'm much closer to the clouds.

"Well, I'll do my best today," he said, pausing to light a menthol cigarette. "But I should tell you that I had to put my dog to sleep two days ago and I'm not in the best of moods."

"I'm sorry to hear that. How old was he?"

"She. She was twelve, almost thirteen."

He bit his lip and took a drag off his cigarette, watching closely as I pulled out a pen and opened a lined notebook that Weiss had provided. Rather than lend me the dictaphone, which would have been much faster, he'd requested that I record everything by hand. In real time, of course, there was no pressing *Pause* and *Rewind,* and I hoped I'd be able to decipher the jerky, racing lines with which I tried to keep up with Jonas Krantz's elaborate answers.

Yet ultimately I was lucky to have been given such a kind and well-meaning subject for my first interview. He listened patiently as I read each question aloud, occasionally stumbling over a word or two, and only once did he ask me to repeat what I'd said. Every now and then his attention seemed to wander as he stared at an empty corner of the room where, I could only assume, his dog used to lie, but it was clear he was making an effort. Whenever his voice trailed off he would shift in his chair and lean forward in order to catch my words, his mouth always slightly open.

Before the interview I hadn't given much thought as to how he would respond but I was surprised by his frequent, if not constant, recourse to metaphor. It was somewhat odd for a scientist, I couldn't help thinking, and by the end I wondered whether he was falling back on an old device, some kind of defense mechanism, circumvention of the truth by way of poetic analogy.

"Do you remember what inspired you to draw the family of ants crossing under the Wall?" had been Doktor Weiss's first question.

Jonas gazed down at his hands, as if what had drawn the ants could testify. "Yes, I remember. I was playing in a small plot of land by the train tracks, filling paper cones with earth. It had just rained and the earth stuck together in clumps. I would grab the clumps and squeeze them until they crumbled. Once the earth was fine enough to run through my fingers I'd pour it into the cones, pretending the grains were gold dust. I'd been playing like this for a while before I noticed all the little ants running about, trying to keep out of my fingers' reach. Without realizing it I'd scooped up a few in a clump of earth, so I quickly released them and they went scurrying in all directions. It seemed so easy for them to just run off like that. And then I thought about how easy it would be for them to cross the Wall. First I thought they could crawl over, but then I realized the journey would seem like Everest so then I thought they could probably just crawl under a point where there weren't too many obstacles below ground."

He shrugged his broad shoulders and lit another cigarette. "Something like that."

"Did you ever feel the same way about birds or bees or butterflies?"

"Definitely not. Ants are imperceptible. Most of the time. Unlike the other creatures you mention. They carry on with their business and no one notices. I always envied them for that."

"And why meteorology? Why did you choose to devote yourself to the study of the atmosphere?"

"It began when I was a child. Around the time I drew the ants. Gazing into the sky was the only activity that gave me a sense of freedom. And I loved predicting what would come next. I trained myself to forecast the weather by reading textbooks, measuring rainfall in jars, recording wind speed with the help of a weather vane. That sort of thing. In the end I'm not sure how successful I was, but each morning I'd announce the day's outlook to my family. Of course, it sometimes meant that my mother would be caught in a downpour without an umbrella or that my brother would go to school without his undershirt, waiting all day for the promised sun to emerge."

"And do you have a special focus?"

"Clouds," he immediately answered. "Definitely clouds."

"Why?"

"Oh, I was quite young," he said. "Nine, I think. I used to pretend to keep a cloud garden, which I fed daily. And when the clouds were big and strong I would unfasten them from their roots and let them drift upward, into the sky, and . . ."

He stopped and again looked down at his hands, which lay folded in his lap.

"And what?"

"Well, I would unfasten them from their roots, but only after months of nurture, during which they prepared for the big ascension, the main event in their lives. Aerial histories were recounted, wind currents and nephological formations explained, navigational skills honed . . ."

He paused again, and laughed quietly. "Sorry, I hadn't thought about my cloud garden in years . . ."

"No, I like it. Tell me more."

"Once in the sky, however," he resumed, "the cloud had to accept that its life would be ephemeral. At best it'd become a rain-laden nimbus and depart in a thunderstorm—and, to everyone but dreamers and meteorologists, it would be indistinguishable from its colleagues."

His expression became more serious.

"And, well, you know, a whole existence might be reduced to drifting upwards to join a cloud rack, merging with the slow-moving flock and then, in a matter of minutes, without having left any imprint on the world, returning to the atmosphere the elements it had been lent."

He stubbed out his cigarette. "Anyhow, these are the things that filled my head when I was a boy."

"And when you grew older, why did you continue with clouds?"

"Oh, for many reasons. Clouds offer insight into the present and, more importantly, into the near future. They're lofty weather stations with frequent changes in staff. And they're generous with their information."

"So mainly for their contents?"

"No, no. The main reason was—or is—the message they offer: all structures are collapsible. Just look at their own existence, condemned to rootlessness and fragmentation. Each cloud faces death through loss of form, drifting towards its death, some faster than others, destined to self-destruct before it reaches the other end of the horizon. After living in the times I've lived in, you create your own concept of flux. Without sounding too simplistic, meteorology helped me understand—and maybe even cope with—recent history, before and after nineteen-eighty-nine. The fogs of time and all the obfuscation that surrounds them."

"How does it feel to belong to a country that only existed, technically, for forty years, eleven months, and three days?"

He shrugged. "The GDR was an artificial creation."

"And do you ever feel nostalgic for those times?"

"Depends on what kind of week I'm having."

"Were your parents in the opposition?"

"Not really. I mean, not actively. My father was a physicist. He had many honors. So they treated him well, for the most part. But that didn't mean he didn't despair. At the drop of a hat you could fall out of favor. He never knew how far up or how low down he was. Everything was so arbitrary, so erratic . . . Again, like the clouds."

"What do you mean?"

"Clouds possess a will of their own yet they live at the constant mercy of air currents."

I must have looked puzzled. He went on.

"I'll give you an example: a cloudling may coalesce one morning and rise to the sky, ready to meander across the horizon for a few hours before joining a bank of other cloudlings. But just as it reaches the right height of the stratosphere and begins to expand, along comes a current of air and blows it in the opposite direction, towards the larger, more self-important clouds, whose protean bodies immediately cast a shadow on the younger one, turning it from fleecy white to downtrodden grey. Even the sky has its pecking order. And when a cloud matures and ceases to soar, its crown dims."

As he spoke, exhaling a few menthol clouds of his own between phrases, I tried to keep up with the analogy. I visualized as best I could the vast network of pawns within the Communist system as if they were clouds in the sky, but it was all too much and by that point my mind was so burdened with cloud images, there was scarcely room for more.

Jonas then told me about his years right after the fall of the Wall, years spent living in various squats in Mitte, running a puppet theater with magnificent wooden puppets a friend had brought from Prague. For those times he was definitely nostalgic, he said, although he had lived hand to mouth, surviving for days on end on nothing but black coffee and pretzels, and during that time he had also suffered a big heartbreak from which it took years to recover, and in the end all the puppets were stolen, one night after a show when his friend forgot to lock up.

In the autumn of 1994 he enrolled at the Humboldt, where he studied mathematics, and later won a scholarship to do a doctorate in meteorology at the Max Planck Institute in Hamburg. The day the letter arrived, he said, was one of two or three that changed his life. He worked sixteen-hour days, got his degree, then moved back to Berlin to become a freelance weather consultant, setting up his own weather station at home.

Forty-five minutes and six cigarettes later (he never offered me any and by the end I was craving one), I closed my notebook and returned it to my bag. The interview had gone smoothly. Jonas Krantz had been generous, even expansive, in his answers, rising to each question with German earnestness and efficiency, and the chair had been comfortable apart from the times I tried to prop up my foot on imaginary rungs.

"If you don't mind my asking, where do you live?" he asked as we walked past a series of weather maps on our way to the door, next to which hung a red leash on a nail.

"Prenzlauer Berg."

"That's not far from here."

"Not really."

"I know this is a little out of the blue," he said, "but what are you doing this Saturday?"

"Going for a walk."

"All night?"

"No, during the day."

"Well, would you like to come to a party that night?"

"What kind of party?"

"Just a party. At an old post office in Mitte."

He wasn't my type but he wasn't bad looking. I had no plans for Saturday. His dog had just died. And with the latest move I'd thrown out my old address book, numbers I used to cling to *just in case*.

So I accepted.

"It was just an idea . . ."

"No, it's fine. I'll come."

I smiled. He smiled. Something was sealed. We agreed to meet outside one of the exits of Stadtmitte U-Bahn at midnight that Saturday.

I was halfway to the elevator when he stuck his head out the door. "You know what, let me take you to the station. It's dark already."

"I'll be fine."

"Are you sure?"

"Yes."

"It's not the safest of neighborhoods."

"I walk fast."

He didn't insist.

The playground was empty, as was the entire communal area, when I emerged from the building, spat out from the fluorescent light of the corridor into the dark street. I buttoned up my coat and walked as fast as I could, this time experiencing a slight shudder as I passed the NPD poster though the moss-covered tombstone was no longer discernable. A few people began to appear as I drew nearer the station and luckily the train pulled into the platform just as I walked up the stairs.

Within the safe confines of the S-Bahn I returned to the last minutes of our conversation. Perhaps it had been wrong to accept Jonas's invitation, I thought to myself, and I should call to cancel. I didn't trust myself. Sometimes I let things go too far, get out of hand, and would then spend months regretting it. I was also unpleasantly reminded of the last time I'd made a date with someone; almost a year ago to the day, it was still fresh in my mind.

I had met him at the newsagents on Greifswalder Straße, where he stood filling out a lottery sheet for the Wednesday and Saturday games, randomly x'ing the squares as if composing an impromptu musical score, while I debated, on the other side of the magazine rack, whether to spend four euros on a new edition of the S-Bahn and U-Bahn map, which featured updated routes and timetables. We were the only two customers in the shop and from across the magazine rack he suddenly said, It's a good map, you should buy it, it's worth the four euros, I have one too and have never arrived late anywhere since. He finished filling out the lottery sheet and handed it to the newsagent, who rung it up and gave him his voucher. How much is the lottery this week? I asked. Two million euros, he and the newsagent answered at the same time. I bought the map and when we left the shop he held the door open and we fell to talking as we walked down the street, then paused before parting ways at the corner near a peeing dog. Dinner sometime? he asked, and I said yes despite finding the pasty skin and lifeless blue eyes far from attractive, but I was impressed by his boldness and thought if nothing else this might be a new friend, so we agreed to meet two days hence at a Thai restaurant near Hackescher Markt, a place I'd never been to but had heard recommended, at eight thirty. I doubt we need to reserve, he said, Just look for me there, I will arrive a few minutes early to find us a table.

But he did not arrive early, and when I turned up in my black corduroy jeans and new purple sweater the restaurant was buzzing with people and the only table left for two was by the window, not a bad location but a little claustrophobic, since the windows were tinted and you couldn't see out. The young Thai waiter was extremely polite and solicitous and brought me the wine menu, which I studied with feigned expertise. I ordered a Riesling, debating for only half a second between a glass and a bottle but promptly deciding on the bottle since it might prove to be a long evening and it was best to be prepared. The bottle was brought, a fine Riesling with a gold seal on the neck, and the waiter poured me a glass which I immediately began to sip while looking around at the other tables. No one seemed to be looking my way yet I felt certain that at least some people noticed the young woman in the purple sweater sitting alone in front of two menus and a full bottle of wine. I studied the label on the bottle, seeing whether there were any words in German I still didn't know, and there was indeed one, which now slips my mind, and as the minutes went by I also read the restaurant menu until I'd studied it to death, flipping through its greasy pages as I counted the number of vegetarian options, and served myself another glass of wine while making a mental note of which starter and main course to order, plus a dessert, green ice cream with toasted coconut shavings—in case there was room.

I lowered my hand under the table to check my watch so no one would notice I was being kept waiting and saw that it was already ten past nine. The boy, whose name I'd forgotten though I'm sure he told it to me on the street corner near the peeing dog, had yet to appear and in order to kill time I hailed the waiter and asked for change for a five-euro bill and went to buy a pack of blue Gauloises from the cigarette machine near the bathrooms, though I'd quit two years before. Back in my seat I asked the waiter, ever present, for an ashtray and matches, then lit the first cigarette, holding it under the table between puffs in order to keep the smoke from blowing in the direction of an elderly couple eating curry to my right. A few minutes later the waiter returned to see whether I wanted to order a starter. Thank you, I remember saying, Thank you but I will wait for my friend, and served myself another glass of wine, after which I checked the door with a discreet turn of the head, pretending to admire the restaurant décor, to see whether there was any sign of him. I again checked my watch under the table: twenty past nine. I began, reluctantly, to face that maybe, just maybe, my dinner companion was not coming after all. But I had this bottle of fine Riesling in front of me, which I would have to pay for no matter what, with no one to split the bill, and so I poured myself one last glass and closed the menu, which I'd intentionally left open so that if the guy walked in and began apologizing I could calmly say, No worries, I was just studying the menu.

With the third, or fourth, glass of wine plus another cigarette, I began to feel the onset of a headache and my temples throbbed just a little, no surprise considering I'd had two thirds of the bottle, maybe more. I extracted a twenty-euro bill from my wallet and paid the waiter the next time he appeared, and at a moment when the people around me seemed particularly engaged in conversation or gluttonously absorbed in their food,

I stood up and walked towards the door, leaving behind the
pack of cigarettes, of which I'd smoked only two but could feel
a sore throat coming on, and as I passed the wooden bowl filled
with restaurant visiting cards I picked one up though I knew
I'd never be coming back, a shame since the food looked good
and I'd known exactly what to order.

That was my last failed date, possibly my karma if such
a thing existed, for I'd stood up a few people myself, twice in
Berlin and also back in Mexico during my volatile teens (I
once sent my sister Yvonne in my place and she ended up
married to the guy for two years). This failed date with the
lottery player had been, for a few weeks thereafter, an item
of neurotic fixation. I couldn't explain why I kept returning
to it, most likely it would have led to nothing, yet it represented some kind of mental unshoring, an ugly confirmation
of what my life in Berlin had become: solitary and inert,
vulnerable to small setbacks. It wasn't an industrious kind
of solitude like Doktor Weiss's but rather a stagnant, infer-
tile one, which bred only more stagnation and infertility. But
I had now decided to give someone else a chance, one small
chance, or perhaps I was giving myself another chance to see
what would happen, or perhaps I was just curious to look
further into what kind of man this ant illustrator turned
meteorologist had become.

On afternoons when the sky was especially clear the television tower's metallic sphere would catch the sun's rays and hover like a spacecraft over Alexanderplatz. At times like these the tower exuded an air of otherworldliness, more extraterrestrial than mystical. It wasn't the eye of God beaming down; if anyone were going to descend from its heights, it would be a cement-trunked alien with a brass ball for a head rather than a robed creature with a halo. Weiss had never mentioned the tower in his writings. Alexanderplatz came up often, as did Socialist architecture and other displays of GDR grimness and grandeur, but the 365-meter monument, oddly, had yet to make an appearance.

The rays of the sun caromed nicely off the television tower but were brought to a halt upon hitting the steel of the gawky cranes that populated the square, although I was pleased to note a gradual and welcome deforestation. Every few days there seemed to be one less crane in Alexanderplatz as their jibs and booms were dismantled and carted off, and I could now cut a clear path from the tram to the S-Bahn to the revamped department store without feeling as if I were crossing an obstacle course of shaky planks and quicksands of rubble. It was a perpetual construction site, Alexanderplatz, and I wondered whether during my lifetime, or at least during my time in Berlin, the day would come when developers would just *let it be*, and I also wondered, every now and then, how much more of the GDR had to be rubbed out before the drills and the shovels and the blueprints would be laid aside, before places like the Palast der Republik and who knows how many other Socialist buildings and landmarks, beautiful and unbeautiful, would stop being gutted or simply erased from the city map.

Doktor Weiss had been delighted with Jonas Krantz's answers. "Clouds. Artificial creations," he read out, unable to suppress a smile. "Well, the boy does have a point."

I realized that in his mind Krantz had remained the six-year-old ant drawer. "And I like his analogies. He seems like a sensible human being, albeit a dreamer."

I confirmed this.

"Tatiana, you did a fine job."

As far as I was concerned, I hadn't done much aside from read aloud his questions and scribble down Jonas Krantz's answers, which I later typed out, but it seemed I'd done enough right for my employer to feel sufficiently confident to assign me another interview, that coming Friday, with someone from the Operations Board of the BVG, Berlin's public transport system.

On my way back from work that afternoon I walked, as was my custom, from the Alexanderplatz S-Bahn to the tram stop to catch the M4 tram that would carry me home. A few cranes dotted the horizon and in the distance the doors to the department store swung open and shut.

As I waited at the shelter counting down the minutes till my tram, I spotted a female figure by the Deutsche Bank cash machines across the tracks, a woman whose quiet brightness stood out against the hectic *toing* and *froing*. My tram was approaching but I decided to take the next one and crossed over to where she stood to study her, discreetly, from closer up. She was in her early to midthirties I would say, with fair skin and ruddy cheeks, and wore a red bandanna tied at the chin, her blonde wispy bangs giving her a lighthearted and almost childlike air. She had on a purple and green flower print dress, a yellow slip hanging out from below, and blue opentoed plastic slippers with thick white socks. What struck me the most about the young woman, however, was her smile. It was wide, open and unchecked, and yet, directionless. She smiled into the air, into the sky, into the city, without seeming to focus on anything or anyone, smiling to herself as if clinging to a compliment or a joke uttered long ago. I also noticed that she had several plastic bags slung over one arm and in the other was holding a bare branch.

A young man walked past on his way to the cash machines. She extended her left palm towards him and opened it up like a flower but he ignored the timid plea. A teenage girl walked past and also ignored her open hand. Four people came and went before she noticed me and promptly held out her hand in my

direction, mumbling a few words in a language I couldn't iden-
tify. I dropped a two-euro coin into her pale palm, admiring the
bright plastic rings on several of her fingers, and the young
woman mumbled a few more words, smiling while she spoke,
her mouth caught between language and whatever the impulse
was that made her smile. The smile seemed to *get in the way of
language*, and she reminded me, I couldn't help it, of a village
idiot who'd been plucked from a small, medieval town and
dropped down unawares in the heart of a bustling city.

From that day onwards I christened her the Simpleton
of Alexanderplatz, and each time my tram passed the Deutsche
Bank cash machines I would look out the window and see her
standing at her post in her flowered dress with her plastic bags
and bare branch, smiling at nothing, smiling *no matter what*.
Every now and then I would walk over to where she was and
drop a few euros into her upturned hand, a pale, clammy micro-
cosm of Alexanderplatz itself with its junctions and fissures,
the city's microbes all gathered in the tip of the index finger,
the atmospheric pressure weighing down the ring finger, the
pinky turned slightly outwards like a crooked weather vane
or a wayward crane. She usually wore her plastic rings, the kind
that came in hollow chocolate eggs, two on one hand and three
on the other.

The more often I saw the Simpleton the more integral
to the landscape she became, as if she'd sprouted from the
cement and was literally rooted to the spot. Armed with her
bags and branch, there she stood in her red bandanna and flow-

ered dress and blue open-toed slippers with thick white socks, people hurrying past her to the machines, sauntering back counting their bills. Yet her invisibility did not seem to bother her, nor did it seem to bother her if it rained, as she simply covered her head with a plastic bag, nor if a strong gust of wind knocked the branch from her hand, which I saw happen twice. I had the feeling her home was far from her daytime haunt and that she traveled a long way to come stand near the Deutsche Bank cash machines at Alexanderplatz, but that was pure speculation. She might have lived in a Plattenbau from whose window she could look out every morning at the four-foot-square area she was about to occupy.

Before interviewing the man from the Operations Board of the BVG I had to transcribe another passage, this one on the *Geisterbahnhöfe* or ghost stations, as West Berliners called the dimly lit, disused stations in East Berlin, which the West Berlin U-Bahn and S-Bahn trains used to cross without stopping.

On August 13, 1961, Berliners were amazed to wake up and find barbed wire fences (eventually replaced by concrete) sealing the border between the Soviet sector and the three Western ones. With the division of the city, its public transportation system, like everything else, was cut in two, yet not without difficulty since the Wall, far from being a neat line down the middle, meandered this way and that. The stations became ghosts at places where the city was not neatly split and Western trains had to cross sections of the East in order to continue their journey to other destinations in the West.

And so it was, Doktor Weiss explained, that this dimly lit Netherworld, frozen in time for nearly thirty years, was created. Each ghost station had its own somber mood and idiosyncrasies, walled-up exits and entrances, and sealed corridors (as if life itself could be immured), but there were a few common features: rampant dilapidation (mountains of bricks, dripping ceilings, peeling plaster), fluorescent bulbs that cast a meager light, and the ubiquitous presence of armed men, green-clothed sentinels watching over a place no one wanted to enter but most wanted to leave.

When shortly after the fall of the Wall, in November 1989, researchers and city planners and other curious folk descended into this land of spirits they found ads, signs, ticket counters and snack bars waiting where they had been left twenty-eight years earlier. The underground Imbiß at the Oranienburger Straße station was a compendium of abandonment: overturned bottles, crushed cans, stained paper cups, counters thick with dust, rusty racks where small bags of peanuts and potato chips once hung, a moldy refrigerator that had been unplugged, severed, like everything else, from its life current in 1961. Faded posters advertising obsolete products, their edges peeling away from the walls to which they clung, their sticking power nothing but sheer obstinacy. Crinkled aluminum foil and soiled wax paper that had wrapped sandwiches digested long ago, a sink choking on fallen plaster, power cords and light fixtures protruding from walls like dangling guts.

The ticket counters, Weiss said, were also trapped in time. One service area, near the Russian embassy, boasted five centimeters of dust and half a dozen brittle rolls of red paper tickets for rides on a defunct transport system. Everything had lain for decades in penumbra and neglect, relics of former days buried under the weight of the Communist regime.

As for the men guarding these stations, in photographs they too seemed like relics of the past. Their faces exuding a subterranean pallor, they were spectral, phantasmal, as if nourished by the weak light of the fluorescent lamps, fed by snatches of passing trains and feeble volts of electricity. They had mutated into a new, strange species, these guards, caged in time like the signs on the walls. Semidarkness, semiconsciousness, semibeing. Theirs was a world of dead silence and dead stillness, blitzed, every now and then, by trains from the West hurtling through their muffled realm. The guards in green watched these trains through narrow glass slits. They spent hours and hours down there, amidst walls pockmarked with age, chairs with soiled cushions and thermoses of watery coffee.

Many of the signs in these stations, Weiss went on to say, were in an old typeface resembling Gothic script: bold black letters, angular and curling upwards like pointed arches or flying buttresses. The signs for Potsdamer Platz and Unter den Linden, perfect examples. As for the peeling advertisements, these showed Teutonic families with cartoonish smiles promoting soap, technical apparatuses or concerts long ago heard, discussed and forgotten. Yet down in the depths of the ghost stations these happy families were only there to tease: no one would have needed soap or music or electrical gadgets, nor would they have been smiling had they brushed against the high voltage rails from which the protective shields had been removed or if they had landed on the metal spikes bristling along the tracks.

As for the West Berliners passing through in their trains, many of them, over time, became desensitized and stopped looking out. Others felt like Orpheus crossing the Underworld, forced to continue on a path without looking back. It was an eerie experience, Weiss said, to travel through this hushed realm where even the lights had been muted to a whisper.

Apart from the delight of listening for hours to a mesmeric voice, it was a blessing to work at my own desk in an empty room in Weiss's apartment, infinitely more pleasing than working at the library, which I'd had to do on occasion in the past, as recently as for my last job at the psychology magazine, and though libraries were fine places in themselves, the finest of places, actually, I always found it impossible to complete the tasks I had been assigned for the simple reason that the more often I went there the more aware I became of the other readers, and the more aware I became of the other readers the more I noticed the profusion of nervous tics and compulsive behavior which seemed to flourish in these places. Pretty soon it was impossible to concentrate on anything, what with the girl to my right chewing her nails and the girl to my left digging at her head, and it did not take long to realize that most people are fidgeters, as if synaptic activity were encouraged by endless scratching and fidgeting, and before long I had the impression I was in a room with eighty scholarly monkeys, busily delousing as they sat reading their books or typing at their computers, and at those rare moments when I looked up and no one was doing anything I felt as if a truce had been called or an angel were flying overhead and, out of deference, the monkeys had removed their paws from their faces and hair.

It was therefore nothing less than paradisiacal to have a desk of my own in a hermetically sealed room with only my employer nearby, and with him, anyway, it was different from the start: I was intrigued, more than a little, wondering how many hours he slept at night and what sort of things he dreamed, what he ate for breakfast and whether he read the labels on cereal boxes and tea bags, what kind of books he kept by his bed, poetry or history or none at all, which items of mail he would open and which he'd toss straight into the bin. I wondered whether he had ever been in love and if so, for how long and with whom, whether he kept a journal or stuck to the recording of "greater" historical events, and how often, if ever, I would cross his mind once I'd finished my transcriptions and gone home for the day. The less information, the more I wanted. I felt like I hadn't even seen his face from all angles yet, just from head-on and one or two quarter profiles, and each time he addressed me I found myself surveying his features with lightning speed like a scanner given only one chance to record an image, the matted eyebrows always coming first, as if asserting their autonomy from the rest.

Every now and then we had an awkward exchange, as on the day he asked about my "papers," a matter that was quickly cleared up although it showed me that I too remained a question mark for him. He had seemed uneasy that morning, as if gearing himself up for an unpleasant task, tightening the belt of his robe, tightening it again although it scarcely seemed necessary, clearing his throat, which didn't sound like it needed clearing. Reading his behavior as some kind of summons, I saved what I had entered on the computer and rose from my seat.

"Tatiana," he said, stalling for a moment once we were face-to-face, "are all your papers in order?"

"Which papers?" I asked, glancing at my desk to see if it looked untidy.

"Your immigration papers. That sort of thing."

"Yes, everything is in order," I answered immediately.

"Are you sure?"

"Yes."

"Good. I'm too old to deal with problems of that sort, and I'm sure you have better things to worry about as well. Work papers, residency papers, everything?"

"Yes, everything," I repeated.

"Good. I'm pleased to hear that. Very pleased. I won't trouble you any further." He again tightened the belt of his robe, as though the act of doubting had loosened it, and left the room, closing the door behind him.

Of course my papers were in order, I muttered to myself as I sat back down. Of course they were in order. When I first arrived in Berlin there were few things I feared more than run-ins with the German police and bureaucracy. From the moment I set foot in the city I made sure to draw as little attention to myself as possible. Of course my papers were in order. It would have taken a real blow on the head for me to forget all my visits to the *Landeseinwohneramt,* the bleak concrete building where I went every two years to renew my visa. How could I forget the industrial wasteland of enormous trucks, factories and warehouses, not a single human face in sight, which one had to cross in order to reach the building to which every *Ausländer* in Berlin was directed? How could I forget walking down its squalid salmon-pink corridors and, even with an appointment, being shown to a waiting room filled with young Turks, Russians and Africans slouched on rows of scuffed white metal chairs bolted to the floor lest someone be seized by the desire to carry one home, and fixing my eyes on the plastic board that listed rooms 11, 10 and 12, in that order, and waiting for someone to call out my name? The buildup to the meeting with the immigration people was always more dramatic than the meeting itself, and the doors to the offices were a frosted glass through which you could see the fuzzy outline of someone moving on the other side, like a poorly executed shadow play, and every now and then the outline would swell in size and the knob would turn and someone would emerge, either the official or else a foreigner whose fate was written across his or her face. Often I'd have to wait for over an hour and would visit the bathroom at least once, although each time I went I cursed the seatless toilets and the stench that made the experience far from neutral, as if the uninviting bathrooms and the squalid salmon-pink corridors were whispering *Reconsider, reconsider,* to every *Ausländer* in search of a visa, and the only redeeming feature I remember from my visits to the bathroom was some of the graffiti on the doors of the stalls. On one of these doors, I remember, was a list scrawled in black marker, providing reasons why not to stay in Germany. I don't recall them now, but after Weiss asked me about my papers I couldn't help remembering this list in the bathroom stall, a place I didn't linger in for long before returning to the waiting room, and the plastic board, and the metal chairs, and by then my senses were so frayed that every name called out had begun to sound like my own, mispronounced in a new way. Of course my papers were in order. That was the least I could pride myself on, my papers were *always in order*, unlike my brother Gabriel, who, even with his handsome bank account and detailed plans for importing bottles of mezcal to the American northeast was sent back to Mexico on the first plane out of JFK.

I was excited about my second interview but from the start fate conspired against me. I'd slept poorly the night before— the usual banging and creaking, along with especially bright cracks of light entering the room—and as a result the next morning my thoughts were scattered and everything took much longer than usual. I didn't have time to dry my hair, still damp from a late shower, and ate in a hurry. I threw on my clothes and quickly changed my canvas bag for a small purse, figuring that the purse would look more elegant and professional. After all, I was going to interview someone high up on the Board of Operations at the BVG.

Herr Dieter Tuchy was friendly at first. He had heavily lidded blue eyes and manicured hands, I noticed from our handshake, and had been employed by the BVG for nearly thirty years. During GDR times he had driven trains through Eastern and Western territory and had since worked his way up. He knew Berlin's transport system, past and present, he said, like the back of his hand. His office was on the top floor of a building directly behind Alexanderplatz, a tiny windowed room with views of the trains running below. After a polite exchange, something about the uncannily warm

afternoon, Herr Tuchy said, "Well then, let's begin. Unfortunately, there's emergency tram work up in Pankow and as
a result one of my colleagues has called a meeting at three.
That means we have approximately forty minutes."

"That should be fine," I said, recalling how easily Jonas
Krantz's interview had gone.

I reached into my purse and pulled out a pen. I plunged
my hand back in and rummaged around, then rummaged some
more, and to my horror realized that my notebook with Doktor
Weiss's questions was in my other bag, the large canvas one,
which I'd left lying on the sofa at home. In my haste I'd forgotten to transfer everything from one bag to the other. I tried to
appear calm as I patted my coat pockets and again searched the
small purse, hoping that by some flourish of magical thinking
the notebook, or at least the paper with Weiss's questions, would
appear.

No such luck. I would have to improvise. And ask for
paper.

"Would you have a few spare pieces of paper by any
chance?"

Herr Tuchy looked surprised. "Well, yes, I suppose I
would . . ." He walked over to his printer, opened the drawer,
and pulled out a stack.

"Oh, that's too much. I only need a few pages, five or so."

He halved the stack and returned the rest to the printer
drawer. It was still too much but I thought it best not to fuss.

"Here you go."

Fortunately, I remembered Weiss's first question. But only the first.

"So, you started out at the BVG as a train conductor for the West Berlin U-Bahn. Line 6."

"Correct."

"What was it like?"

"What was what like?"

"What was it like to drive through the ghost stations?"

He shrugged his shoulders. "After a while you stopped noticing. You just looked in front of you, at the tracks."

"And what would you see?"

"Tunnel. Tracks lit by the lights of the train. More tunnel."

From there on, it was time to improvise. I racked my brain trying to think of questions a historian would ask.

"Were you always very aware of the divided city?"

"I was getting on with my job. What was I supposed to do each time we drove through? The guards on the platform never waved hello."

"I see."

Herr Tuchy looked out the window at an intercity train pulling up to a platform and then back at me, ready for the next question.

"And, um, did you ever feel there were actual ghosts, or spirits, in these ghost stations?"

"Of course not. There was nothing supernatural about them. Calling them ghost stations romanticizes what they really were. They just happened to lie in disuse."

"And darkness."

"Yes."

My mind raced, trying to think of another question. "And, um, why didn't these stations appear on the East Berlin subway maps?"

"Why would they?"

I tried to visualize the sheet of paper I'd printed out and the vertical row of questions, but all I drew was a blank.

Herr Tuchy glanced at his watch.

"And . . . weren't the guards bored down there?"

He shrugged. "It was their job."

"Didn't they grow pale? Deprived of light?"

"It was their job."

"Could they even *see* down there? Wasn't it very dark?"

"Their other senses were sharpened. They could hear a pin drop."

By the time the interview drew to a close my relief must have been palpable. I had asked twelve questions and received twelve answers, albeit not the ones I had been sent to ask. Herr Tuchy checked his watch a second time. Our forty minutes were up.

As we began walking towards the door, a thought occurred to me.

"I have one last question, actually."

"Yes?"

"The voice on the S-Bahn, that's a recording, right?"

"Yes, of course."

"Made by a real person?"

"Yes, of course."

"And when was it recorded?"

He closed his eyes for a few seconds in order to access some file at the back of his mind, then reopened them. "In 1997."

"So all the S-Bahn recordings were done in 1997?"

"Yes, at a studio near Hamburg."

"By the same person?"

"Yes, of course."

"Is he an actor or does he work for the BVG?"

"I thought our interview was over."

"It is. But could you just tell me quickly: actor or BVG employee?"

"I'm sorry, but . . ."

"Is he as young as he sounds or has he aged beyond his voice?"

"I'm sorry, I must prepare for my meeting."

Another firm handshake, this time nearly crushing my little finger. German steadfastness, an invincible opponent; it was time to step down.

I hoped Weiss would never hear about my final round of questions but it was unlikely that he would, unless Herr Tuchy decided to issue a complaint. I assumed he was far more concerned with the emergency tram work in Pankow, which I hoped the BVG would promptly attend to since it would affect my routes as well.

On my way home I spotted the Simpleton, standing there clutching her branch, this one with flowers sprouting from one end. Slung over her other arm was an assortment of plastic bags, white, blue and beige. She had changed her dress, I noticed. This one was also flowered, but had a little blue collar, as far as I could tell as the tram passed at 19.2 kilometers an hour, and was notably shorter than the previous dress, drawing attention to her knock-knees and skinny thighs. She had on the same plastic open-toed slippers from which protruded thick white socks. Her bandanna and her smile were also in place, as perfectly in place as everything else, and I felt like smiling back as we passed her small, insignificant figure posted there, a meter away from the Deutsche Bank cash machines. I doubted that the Simpleton and Herr Tuchy ever crossed paths, despite spending their days within the same small circumference of Alexanderplatz, he, she, and the television tower, all collecting similar molecules of sun and smog and city hysteria.

On days when it rained I would think of a man I once knew, one of my early acquaintances in Berlin, who in his delirium would try to stop the rain from falling. Each time it rained he would cease whatever he was doing and rush out into the street, often quiet streets without much traffic, and start hitting the drops upwards, slapping them back into the sky. It was a pointless campaign against gravity, but he said he wanted to return the rain to the heavens, to the place where it belonged. I never found out whether he responded similarly to snow; before winter he packed up and moved to Antwerp.

Mornings and afternoons when the Simpleton wasn't there Alexanderplatz seemed silent and empty, like an engine without a hum or a sea without its algae. At that point in my life she and Weiss were the only human beings I saw more or less regularly, though my communication with both was, needless to say, limited, at least until the day of the sixty-watt bulb, which in retrospect was a turning point in my relations with my employer. He hadn't been as annoyed as I feared he would be after my interview with the BVG man, nor was he entirely pleased. Some of my questions were fine and close to his own, but others, apparently, were either way off track or redundant.

"Now why would I want to know about how pale the guards were? I *know* they were pale, what more information does one need?" he asked.

"I thought . . ."

"You thought what? I am the one who thinks. You transcribe."

A few days later, I was in the midst of transcribing a passage on the "Baedeker Bombing," as Berliners sometimes called the Allied air raids of 1945 that pulverized historical buildings and other former tourist attractions, when the bulb in the overhead light began to flicker. The day had been grey and overcast, the weak, tired sun barely managing to penetrate the windowpane: a rare instance that called for artificial light. I dragged my chair over to the hanging lamp, climbed up and tapped the bulb with a pencil. It flickered three final times and then went out. I turned off the switch, unscrewed the bulb, and shook it, listening to what sounded like loose tinsel rattling around inside. There was no doubt that the bulb was blown and in order to continue working I would have to ask my employer for a replacement. This would be the first time I interrupted him yet I had no choice but to cross the corridor and knock on his door, which opened almost immediately.

"Yes?" Weiss's body filled most of the frame. Beyond his shoulders all that was visible were the corners of bookshelves and a lamp with a green shade.

"The bulb in my room went out. I think it needs to be changed."

"I should have more bulbs in the kitchen."

"Should I . . . will you . . . ?"

"Come," he said, closing the door to his study behind him.

I followed him down the corridor, neither of us making a sound, and through a door that had yet to be opened in my presence. On the other side lay the kitchen, a brown-tinged space with a table and two chairs, an old chrome refrigerator, and a long counter with a fitted stove, sink and cabinets. On the counter, beside an empty wine rack, stood various kitchen appliances, a blender, a toaster and a food processor, all covered in thick, furry dust. A small espresso maker with a melted black handle sat on the stove. Weiss crouched down before a set of cabinets beneath the sink.

"Would you like some help?"

He didn't answer, though the screech of the cabinet door as he tugged it open sounded like a reply, and started to forage through whatever was down there.

Light steps, announcing a black smudge, entered the kitchen from another door at the back. The steps drew nearer, the figure came into focus. The black smudge morphed into a small four-legged creature and unless I was imagining this, it was the Xolo, the very same Xolo I had seen outside Bar Gagarin.

"Is that your dog?" I asked incredulously.

"Yes, that's Murci," Weiss answered without looking up.

"I think I've seen him before."

The dog walked towards a set of bowls by the wall and then paused, as if suddenly made aware of someone new in the room and just as on the day at the café he changed direction and came to sit before me, pinning his dark eyes on my own. I was astonished to see him again, but my astonishment was all the greater upon realizing that the dog had recognized me, or else, sensing I was one of his own, had had the same impulse, both times, to approach.

Doktor Weiss rose from his crouching position and smoothed out his robe. "I don't seem to have any more bulbs. Is the room too dark otherwise?"

"I can try. . ." I said, before repeating, "I think I've seen your dog before."

"We rarely leave the house."

"Do you ever go to Bar Gagarin?"

"Gagarin? Never."

"It's next door to Pasternak, near the Wasserturm."

"I know Pasternak."

"Would you have gone there, with the dog, in late August?"

"Possibly."

"One Sunday, the day after that big summer storm?"

"We may have gone to Pasternak the day after the storm. It's possible."

"Well then, I saw your dog. I saw him and I thought he

was lost and I wanted to bring him home but he disappeared. I've thought about him many times since."

Weiss glanced at his dog, then back at me.

"Why's he called Murci?"

"It's short for Murciélago. He looks more like a bat than a dog."

"Did you bring him from Mexico?"

"A friend did. Germany's leading authority on Alexander von Humboldt."

As if remembering his mission, the dog rose from his sitting position and walked over to his bowls, returning to the status of a black smudge, and started eating.

"What do you know about this Wasserturm?" Weiss asked.

"I've never been inside but I think there are apartments, maybe a gallery."

I'll never know what prompted Weiss at that moment to offer me a seat and something to drink. Perhaps it was curiosity, or mere resignation, for without light I wouldn't be able to complete my work that day, or perhaps it was a friendly impulse inspired by Murci's presence, but there was no doubt a shift. Without any hesitation I accepted and watched as he poured elderflower syrup into two glasses and added water from a bottle in the refrigerator. In contrast to the measured tone he used for the dictaphone, his movements were brisk and he left a puddle of syrup on the counter.

"Ice?"

"No, that's fine."

He brought the two glasses over to the table and vigorously stirred their contents with a spoon, spilling a few drops of each. We drank. The drink was tremendously sweet; he must have gotten carried away with the syrup.

"That Wasserturm, Tatiana, was built by the English Waterworks Company in 1856. In 1933 it was used by SA troops for holding and torturing anti-Fascist prisoners. And now it is used, as you say, for apartments 'with a nice view of the square' and for those pseudoartistic spaces that have spread through Berlin like a virus."

"I thought it had just been a water tower."

"Don't you read the plaques outside of buildings? That demon of brick shouldn't be used for anything new. Can you imagine if someone opened a café at the Topography of Terror site, with an espresso machine chugging away in one of the torture cells, right there at the very headquarters of the Gestapo and the SS? It'd be nearly as outrageous as what they did with the villa where the Wannsee conference was held, which, *for thirty-six years* after the war, was used as a hostel for inner-city children. Imagine the sort of energy those children imbibed, playing games in the room where the 'Final Solution' for getting rid of every single Jew in Europe was laid out to top Reich administrators, or going for a dip in the tainted waters of the lake or for a run through the rose garden with its sinister miniature roses, so well tended, always blooming; after that, Wannsee should've been renamed *Wahnsinn*, it would have been much more fitting."

Weiss paused. "Everything here is shifting and shifting but you can't forget it all forms part of one long continuum."

I finished my drink. He got up, refilled the glass with syrup and water, and sat down again, this time forgetting to stir. By now the Xolo had finished eating and was curled up like a lump of coal by the stove.

"I could tell you many stories," he said, "but you would view them as the senile musings of an old historian who has seen his city change face many times."

"Well, I have a story I can tell you," I said without thinking.

"About what?"

"About something, or rather someone, I saw in Berlin in 1986."

Encouraged by the more intimate context in which we now found ourselves and coasting on the high from the elder-flower syrup, I told the historian, in one long rush of words, about the night I saw Hitler on the U-Bahn. I told him about the demonstration against the Wall and the way everyone had lit candles and lighters (he'd been there too, but had left by dusk), and about the dizzying heat on the subway and about my frustration with my family for not having seen what I had.

Throughout my account his expression remained blank, impossible to read, and as I drew to a close I began to worry that

I'd said something wildly inappropriate. He was silent for a few moments and then, lifting his head from the hand on which it had been resting, said, "August 1986. He would have been ninety-seven by then. Did this woman look ninety-seven to you?"

"Yes, she looked almost a hundred."

"The age tallies."

He fell silent again, his eyebrows lowered in thought, and, a tense minute or two later, he said, "And yet I'm sorry to say, I don't believe your story."

"I'm not making it up."

"It's transference of some kind. Hallucination. Projection. Call it what you will."

Projection. It was too easy to attribute every wrong step, every false hope, every crushed fantasy, every mislaid faith, to projection. The three syllables made me wince. But I sat politely in my chair, took another sip of the sweet water, and nodded.

"No, Tatiana," he continued, "you experienced what one could call the Hitler syndrome. Over time one realizes that Hitler is everywhere. His spirit is just as much in the body of that bluebottle fly there on the windowpane as it was in the old woman you saw on the U-Bahn as in this ballpoint pen lying on the table. He's just as much in that sparrow on the branch as in the insect in the sparrow's beak."

"But it was him that day. I'm sure it was. He was still alive, and in Berlin. It wasn't a delusion."

Weiss shook his head. The shock of hair usually brushed to the side fell into his face. He left it there.

If only I could have better described the sensation of seeing the old woman in the scarf surrounded by her grey buzzards and the way she'd stared back, trying to soften me with her smile, and the stifling heat in the carriage and how even in the midst of all the confusion and my disorientation, how real this one vision had been, but no, it hadn't been a vision, it had leapt out with the starkness of black and white against the hubbub of color, and that was part of the problem, I thought to myself, all those war documentaries one saw in black and white, when of course history, like life, took place in color, although in our memories the color was usually removed, and now even my memory of that old hag on the U-Bahn escorted by her cronies had faded to the monochrome of museum photographs and history reels.

Weiss checked his watch. I took the cue and rose from my seat.

"Don't bother bringing the glasses to the sink, I need the exercise," he said.

Despite the awkward note on which it ended, after that afternoon I sensed there was a small aperture, a tiny passage through which more human feeling now flowed. Even if Weiss hadn't believed my story he seemed to take me more seriously, or at least be more aware of my presence. He studied me often, I noted, and with curiosity, and raised my salary to eighteen euros an hour. Yet the hierarchy remained in place, never faltering for a second; he was the distinguished historian and I the hired scribe, and even at moments when he assumed a faintly warm, avuncular posture he quickly checked himself and returned to gruffness, like an old cat unable to retract its claws.

On my way over to meet Jonas for our so-called date, I realized that the main reason I had accepted was simply in order to avoid yet another feeling of *what if* to add to the long chain of other *what if*'s in my life, a chain that grew heavier as the years went by, and as the U-Bahn lurched from one station to the next, bringing me closer and closer to the person I'd arranged to meet, I thought about all my recent and long-past attempts at friendship, not to mention a few rather pitiful stabs at romance, marveling all the while at my astonishing success in sabotaging every relationship I entered. Of course it hadn't always been that way, not when I was young in Mexico, but after crossing the ocean and opting for this exile, I found myself needing other people less and less. Growing up in a household with four siblings had brought with it the misery of shared bedrooms, a cacophony of gulping and slurping at every meal, endless waits for the shower, and many other communal experiences that I was more than happy to leave behind. As a result, space and silence were priceless commodities and upon arriving in Berlin I was thrilled to have my own room and follow my own rhythms and routines. Anything that threatened the established order was unwelcome.

As I sat on the U-Bahn staring out into the darkness of the tunnel, I thought not about my last failed date at the Thai restaurant but about another desperate attempt at friendship, also one of the most laughable. Sonia was her name. Sonia the fitness trainer, who after a few coffees in the neighborhood (we lived on the same street) insisted I visit the gym where she worked, and I, who had never done a lick of exercise in my life apart from P.E. class at school, finally succumbed and even bought a pair of cheap tennis shoes for the occasion. Why go for walks when you can go to the gym, she had said. I like the fresh air, I replied. There's nothing fresh about city air, she'd answered. City air is about the dirtiest air you can breathe. At our gym we have the best air-conditioning system in all of Germany. Now *that's* clean air. I like to watch people, I told her, at which she laughed and said, Nothing is better than people-watching at the gym.

She lent me a pair of sweat pants to go with my T-shirt and tennis shoes and I followed her into the refrigerated gym. Before even looking around my first impulse was to flee, the same impulse I'd had before each P.E. class. But by no means was Sonia going to let me get away and with one flexing of her tiny bronzed muscles she clutched my shirt and pulled me towards a large grey machine with clammy handles, handles that must have preserved the residue of years of human sweat. Not wanting to cause a scene I stepped onto the rotating pedals and seized the handles to steady myself while Sonia punched in some data. Before I knew it I was off, my hands and feet flying as the machine took over, each revolution drawing me more into its rhythm. After a few minutes I actually began to enjoy the glide of the pedals, with every turn another worry seemed to evaporate, and I tried not to think too much about the decades of sweat with which I was coming into contact, remembering instead the words of those who said that exercise was the one true mood enhancer.

Then I started to look around. There was a limited number of directions in which I could turn my head and so I was a captive audience; there, directly in front of me, was a repellently thin man in red shorts and a black tank top lifting weights at a machine. His shoulders jutted out like the ends of a metal hanger, and he looked as though a giant had seized him by the head and toes and gnawed him down like corn on the cob. Each time he lifted the bar he would squeeze his eyes shut and his entire face would turn a reddish purple. Dark blue veins bulged on his arms and legs like roots about to burst from the ground. The sight of him was grotesque and I longed to look away but part of me was drawn to the grotesqueness and I had to keep checking to make sure he was really that skeletal, no more than forty kilos I would say, surprised that his body didn't snap like a twig.

I finally managed to tear my eyes away and forced myself to look at the television monitors hanging from the ceiling, but they were showing a sports channel, and not only was it a sports channel but an equestrian show, the sort of spectacle that had always disturbed me since at every moment I feared the horses would trip over the fences, crash onto their faces and shatter their legs, so my last resort was to look down, away from the monitors and the human stick insect, but there I had the calorie counter telling me how many calories I was burning a minute, and that too began to get in the way of any enjoyment, and as the minutes wore on I broke into a sweat and began to hallucinate black cats perched on the StairMaster machines behind me, but when I looked over my shoulder the cats turned into workout consoles. I don't know how long I lasted, at least twenty minutes or twenty-five, before stepping off. The room spun around and I thought I would faint but I quickly sobered up at the sight of Sonia, whose face could not hide her displeasure, and I was soon to discover that beneath the cheery camaraderie lurked a harder spirit, one for whom most friendships bore an expiration date, and that same evening she coldly announced what I too had been thinking, that we were simply too different to be friends, and apart from living on the same street (and not for much longer, since I was planning to move) we had little, or rather nothing, in common.

I later asked myself what Sonia's inner landscape would have looked like; even the most impoverished of souls, my mother always said, have an inner landscape, and I concluded that hers would have been an empty lot with tennis balls scattered like boulders, punctuated by the occasional peak of a NordicTrack or StairMaster machine. In the end, she represented the last of many attempts, each one more absurd, at some kind of intimacy that went beyond the occasional hello, how are you.

The light outside Stadtmitte station was dim; for once, no aggressive streetlamps rose in arms against the natural darkness of the night. Jonas was waiting on a bench in jeans and a black shirt with pocket flaps when I arrived at ten past midnight. He stood up, kissed me timidly on the cheek, and without another word we began walking toward the party, two steps of mine for each of his long strides. After crossing a few streets we arrived at Krausenstraße, where the old abandoned post office sat.

Drinks were cheap. Beers one sixty, vodka tonics two euros, all served in plastic glasses that easily tipped over. The party organizers had run out of ice and the beer was room temperature but no one seemed to mind. We wove our way through the crowd, mostly scenesters in their twenties dancing to an electronic version of "Love Will Tear Us Apart."

Aside from at the bar, set up in the former package-holding area, most people were gathered in the courtyard, which had been furnished with tattered chairs and sofas fished out of dumps. Within minutes I'd recognized several faces from my going-out days, people I used to observe and occasionally exchange a few words with. There was the short-haired platinum blonde who called herself a journalist though no one had ever seen a word she'd written. There were the two American butterflies, young, pretty girls who flitted from party to party with German boys panting at their heels. There was the Swiss rockabilly who had tattooed the name of every girlfriend he'd had on his neck. I could see there'd been a few additions and he would soon be running out of space. There was the Danish couple with their matching stringy blond hair who spoke a funny mix of English and German. And there they were, without fail, the older couple in their fifties who came to every so-called underground event, tireless pursuers of an era that no longer existed, unable to stay home with the knowledge that every night, *somewhere in town*, there was something "illicit" going on. They stood in their battered leather jackets, puffing on cigarettes, the woman with her screaming red hair and the man with his round glasses and pointy beard and roving lupine expression.

Unable to face more than an hour at home, most of these people had continued to go out every night, rushing to and fro as they exchanged the same cool, noncommittal pleasantries about gigs, eternal job searches and flat swaps, new vintage record and clothing shops, the latest gallery to open, and all the other things that kept Berlin abuzz. I remembered those days too well, days I'd blessedly left behind, I thought to myself as Jonas and I sank into one of the sofas in the courtyard.

We finished our drinks and, fully at ease around each other by now, got seconds. I kept to vodka despite the acrid taste and suspicious generic label, WODKA in slanted red letters against a white background. The bar had run out of glasses so we hung on to the ones we had, careful not to tear or crack the flimsy plastic.

"The sky is hard to read tonight," Jonas said. "It's like there's a veil between me and everything up there."

"It looks like the usual night to me. Except we can't see the moon from where we're sitting."

"No, it's more than that. See those clouds up there, the noctilucent clouds? Even they seem more distant than usual. I can't explain . . . I hate it when I can't read the sky," he added. "But it's something I have to deal with. Every now and then it simply withholds its language."

"That's how I often feel with Weiss."

"Not enough communication?"

"Well, most of it is through the dictaphone."

"Why doesn't he write things down himself?"

"He says he's no good at typing."

"What's wrong with pen and paper?"

"I think he likes speaking into his little metal object."

A large man with shoulder-length hair spilling out from under a baseball cap wandered into the courtyard lugging a black case. He looked like a trucker and I wondered whether he was lost since at first he seemed flustered, as if in need of directions. But no, he had found the right address. As soon as they spotted him, the American girls ran up and draped themselves around his neck, two trussed birds strung from the neck of an ox. A guy in tight black jeans materialized by his side to relieve him of his heavy case. Someone else produced a pack of cigarettes and a drink.

"That's Juju the DJ," Jonas informed me. "He just flew in from Prague."

Juju's entourage was swelling by the minute and soon all I could see was the top of his baseball cap. Jonas turned back to me.

"So, what is Weiss working on these days? A book or articles or what?"

"A book, I believe."

"About Berlin?"

I nodded.

"What more can he say? He's written so much about Berlin already. Everyone has. What was the last thing you transcribed?"

"Something about ghost stations."

"Oh, the famous ghost stations . . ."

"Did you know they existed?"

"Of course."

Jonas peeled a large strip of the label off his beer bottle and crumpled it into a ball. "And what does he do with the transcriptions? Surely they're not ready to go to print?"

"I'm not sure. He's never said."

He had a good point. I actually had no idea what happened once the historian received the pages I'd transcribed. He must go through them and . . . File them? Turn them into more fluid prose? And had he always worked this way, hiring transcriber after transcriber? Was I just one in a long line of people who had listened to this voice or was it a new need of his that had arisen with age?

"I heard someone say," Jonas continued, peeling off what was left of the label, "that Weiss has nothing left to write, that he's completely disconnected from the present and only writes about things that have been discussed to death and that his last few articles, I don't think he's published an actual book in a while, offered nothing new."

"Who said that?"

"My cousin's professor. He teaches history at the Humboldt."

"Well, like I said, I don't know what he's going to do with this stuff."

"You mentioned ghost stations."

"Yes."

"So maybe it's true that Weiss dwells too much on what spaces *were* . . . But Berlin can't just be a museum of horror. There has to be regeneration, don't you think?"

I nodded, though the very act of nodding felt like betrayal. Jonas was silent for a minute, his mouth ajar.

"Well, maybe this historian is wrong and Weiss is indeed contributing something. I'm not passing judgment myself. I've read two of his books. And I really admire the man."

Even with these final words I didn't like the direction in which our conversation was heading so when a new song came on, an extended Rammstein remix with lots of rolling *r*'s, I jumped up and grabbed Jonas's hand. It was quite a sight, Germans dancing, though I was used to it by then. Every now and then there was someone perfectly synchronized with the music, but most of the time I felt like I'd fallen into a colony of robots, each programmed differently and following a separate signal. If you observed them as a group you would never have thought they were responding to the same song.

I hadn't danced in ages but after two or three drinks it didn't matter. Unlike some of his peers, Jonas wasn't a bad dancer and we each did our own thing, occasionally meeting eyes, pretending to be more caught up in what was going on around us than between. Rammstein was followed by Depeche Mode, Depeche Mode by an Italo Disco classic from the early eighties. We kept dancing. And I was actually enjoying myself. It had been months, perhaps years, since I'd gone to a party and lost track of time. After half an hour I usually began checking my watch, counting every wasted minute until I'd finally get my act together to leave.

Jonas Krantz had a sweet, placid manner that somehow neutralized the roar of the land around us and although the things he'd said about Weiss no doubt disturbed me I managed to push them to the back of my mind. I would go over it all tomorrow, there was no need to just now, and after a few minutes I delivered myself to the dance, feeling exhilaration at enjoying something usually off-limits, similar to the way I'd felt while turning around and around on the machine at the gym before certain sights soured the experience. Indeed, the evening would have been one of the most pleasant I'd had in a while had it not been for the strange turn it suddenly took, reality's noose slipped back around my neck.

At two in the morning, done with our dancing, we had replenished our beer and vodka and gone to sit on a shabby couch with protruding springs when a young man appeared before us. I'd been watching him for the past half hour as he approached people in the courtyard, swinging an unlit flashlight as if it were some kind of whip, and I had seen how some of these people had gone to stand near what looked like a trap door in a corner.

Jonas had been in the midst of telling me about his love of weather vanes, particularly the weather vane he had installed on the roof of his building, a replica of a medieval lion with slanted eyes that spun around chasing its tail depending on what direction the wind was blowing, when the man with the flashlight walked over.

"We're starting the tour soon. Would either of you like to come?" he asked, swinging his flashlight.

"What tour?" Jonas inquired.

"Of the Gestapo bowling alley."

"Which?"

"The one here, under the post office. We already have eleven people. We can only bring twelve, so one of you can come. If you want."

"I'll come," I said before Jonas could answer. I wasn't sure whether he'd intended to say yes but I was responding to a strong urge inside, perhaps the voice of my employer, which told me to accept before it was too late.

I'd also heard other people wax lyrical about Berlin's underground world, a whole topography that lay, forgotten, twenty or thirty or forty feet down. Bunkers, theaters, disused this and that, countless tunnels, arches, storerooms and other damp, dark cavities: an architectural miscellany in permanent hiding from the sun. That was Berlin's underground world, but what I was about to descend into, I soon discovered, was more like Berlin's *Unterwelt*. As soon as the rusty door banged shut and our guide flicked on his flashlight I had the urge to flee but curiosity and, oddly enough, a sense of duty, made me stay on, especially given the last things Jonas had said about my employer, for I suddenly felt the need to prove everyone, or at least *someone*, wrong, and so it was that our conversation catapulted me into this impulsive decision.

Our young guide informed us his name was Jörg. He turned to count his sheep, twelve in all, and then shepherded us into a phantasmagoric land where it seemed no living creature had set foot for decades. Instantly, everyone fell into a hush. The only sounds were those of our footsteps and of the moisture dripping in large beads off the walls and ceiling. Jörg told us to stick close together as there was no electricity down here and every chance in the world of getting lost, and also warned that he and the other party organizers would not be held responsible should a large piece of plaster or anything else fall from the ceiling.

There was no doubt that the entire basement lay in great disrepair. I couldn't see the dankness but I could definitely smell it, and I had the uncomfortable sensation that we delegates of the present were intruding on the past, every step of ours widening the incision. Each room we entered had the same dripping ceilings and wires jutting out of the walls at different angles and every now and then Jörg would train his flashlight on a pile of rubble or an especially large iron bar or tangle of wires, bringing these forgotten fragments back to life for a few seconds. Given the ease with which he seemed to know his way around, I assumed he gave this tour often and took pride in his expertise.

After traversing several dark, damp rooms, plowing ever deeper into the labyrinth, though it was hard to tell how many doorways we'd actually crossed, we arrived at the so-called Gestapo bowling alley, a rectangular room, somewhat larger than the others as far as I could tell. Our guide asked us to fan out so that everyone could see and directed his flashlight at different spots. I stepped out from behind a tall girl with pigtails and began to look around. It was a pretty chilling sight. Everything, it seemed, was just the way it had been left decades ago. At the center of the room lay a metal contraption, about eight feet long, an obsolete machine once used for spitting out wooden bowling balls, and with its rusty corners and thin bars, it looked, at least from afar, like a medieval instrument of torture, like those racks to which victims were bound by their hands and feet and then stretched.

On the walls, Jörg pointed out, one could still see the last set of scores written in chalk. Six lines on one side, nine on the other. Small triumphs and defeats, recorded for posterity, scores made by supple, energetic fingers or by cold, stiff ones. I felt certain that we'd just interrupted a game and that the moment we turned around and headed out uniformed phantoms would appear to continue playing.

"Is this definitely a Nazi bowling alley?" someone asked.

"Nazi, Stasi, what's the difference," Jörg answered. "We've always called it the Gestapo bowling alley but no one knows for sure."

So much for historical accuracy, I thought, each of us was as guilty as the next, surrendering to intellectual laxness for the sake of mystery and thrill.

"Well, we'd better head back up now," Jörg said, just as some people began to inch closer to the contraption and others began checking the ceiling for falling bits of plaster although none had yet crashed down. Drops of water fell from the ceiling, drops of the past falling onto the present, and I too was more than ready to return to ground level.

Just as we were leaving the room, however, a fat bead of condensation landed on my forehead and as I wiped it off with my sleeve I was seized by the urge to go back and wipe, with the same simple brush of the sleeve, the bowling scores from the wall. I can't explain why I had this urge, but all of a sudden I felt that I would never forgive myself if I didn't go back and erase these scores made by anonymous victors and losers.

Nazi, Stasi, whatever they were, why the hell should they be
granted this kind of posterity? Let the metal contraption stay
where it was, there wasn't much one could do with it, but as
for the chalk markings, why leave them? Jörg wouldn't notice
if I snuck back for a few seconds, and if I hurried I would still
have enough light from where he was shining his flashlight in
the next room.

      I turned back and walked around the contraption, up to
the wall with the scores. On second thought, I decided to use
my fist rather than my sleeve, so I clenched my right hand and
in one sweeping gesture smudged the lines. Jörg, flashlight and
herd were moving away with plodding determination. Darkness was closing in. I could no longer see enough to gauge how
much I'd erased but the motion itself felt satisfying, as if I were
now having the last word, and I would have to leave it at that.
I turned and headed towards the sound of footsteps, barely
audible now. The bowling alley, this hideous room of recre-
ation, was growing darker by the second. Tones deepened from
grey to dark grey to charcoal to burnt charcoal. Soon it would
be 100 percent undiluted blackness. I could barely see the
outline of the door. But I knew that somehow my feet would
lead me away, back up to the surface. Somehow. I strained
my eyes and took a step forwards and then another and with
the third step I tripped. It was enough of a stumble to make
me lose a few seconds, crucial seconds, and as I hit the ground
I felt the sharp edge of the metal contraption dig into my
thigh.

Something prevented me from crying out. My cries would have been heard, I'm sure, but my fear of drawing attention to myself was, at least during the first few minutes, greater than my fear of being left behind. By now I could barely hear the others. I pushed myself off the ground and limped in what I thought was the direction of the door though I could no longer be sure. My thigh stung and I must've scraped my knees since they began to sting too. I walked into a wall and came face to face with dampness; I turned and headed to my right until I came face to face with another wall, here too almost kissing the cement. My face was perspiring and the wall was perspiring and I could no longer tell whose perspiration was whose. I dried my face with my sleeve. It was becoming clear, all too clear, that I'd been left behind, in this sinister place with not a single coordinate to guide me. Jörg and his flock had trudged away, under the falling plaster and dripping ceilings, like scared sheep fleeing the corpse of a wolf.

What I would have given, at that moment, for a mobile phone. I'd always resisted buying one on the grounds that I was usually at home and when I wasn't at home I had no desire to be contacted. But what I wouldn't have given on that Saturday night for a phone, a phone with which to reestablish contact with the rest of the world, or, even without a signal, a nice little phone with a luminous screen to light my way.

I hoped, or rather, prayed, that Jörg would do a head count once they reached the outside and see that someone was missing. Had he taken much notice of me, I wondered, enough notice to realize that I was no longer part of the group? And what about Jonas Krantz, whose existence I'd completely forgotten this past half hour? Surely he would note that I hadn't reemerged with the rest. Yes, Jonas would be my salvation. He would see I was missing and raise the alarm and send Jörg or someone else down with a flashlight to find me. For the first time in my life I longed for a crack of light, even the slightest hint of illumination, for one small bulb offering artificial splendor of the dimmest sort, a flickering glow to guide me back to civilization. But in cruel answer to my prayers I was, for once, utterly submerged in darkness. And it was terrifying.

On my way down I hadn't paid much attention to how deep we'd come but I now had the impression that I was far below the ground, separated from the rest of humanity by leagues, no, by kilometers, cut off by six or seven decades rather than by five minutes and a couple of meters. I was at the same depth, I reckoned, as the dismal cells where political prisoners were once kept and tortured. What if, I thought to myself with horror, this underground bowling alley were connected via tunnels to the Topography of Terror site, so that the Gestapo men could take a break from torturing prisoners to come knock down a few pins? What I needed, if not a mobile phone to guide me back to the world of the living, was the little black Xolo, to guide my soul, if indeed I was there to stay, to a more beautiful resting place.

Minutes passed and as they did I had the growing impression that I was not alone. I heard a sound from somewhere in the room, the sound of someone breathing, the sound of Gestapo agents coming to resume their game. I could almost feel the rustling of thick grey coats as the gruesome specters returned and tapped their feet, waiting impatiently for this foolish intruder to leave their bowling alley so they could get on with things. Of course they would come back to finish. They now had an eternity to play. The scores I'd erased would shortly be replaced by new scores. Twenty years later, the ghouls I had seen on the U-Bahn continued to linger, only in a new dimension. If they'd stuck around that long there was no reason to think they would leave now. No, they were here to stay, bound to Berlin for an eternity.

Forget the three ladies from below; I was dealing with the serious past now. Weiss would have said the same. Stop thinking about Weiss, I told myself, think about how to find your way back, back to the land of the living. I heard the sound of more breathing and the swish, swish of thick grey cloth, so thick it didn't even dent. The room was getting crowded, the air dwindling, and I felt like Laika, the ill-fated dog the Soviets sent into space, trapped in her capsule as the air heated up and those watching from screens on earth realized there was nothing they could do to save her. More footsteps, hurried, approaching from another room. A light shone in. Just in time. Five minutes more and I would probably have fainted or given myself a heart attack. Jörg appeared, followed by another guy. I nearly wept when I saw them.

*   *   *

A live band had replaced the eighties music and when I found Jonas he was dancing with a girl in low-cut jeans and a mullet. He held out a can of beer, urging me to take a sip. I shook my head and limped away. He looked puzzled but kept dancing. One of the people who'd been on the underground tour with me came up to ask what had happened. I told her I'd lost my way. She asked me if I'd been scared. I lied.

After a few minutes Jonas came to look for me. He asked how the tour had gone.

"Okay," I told him.

"Just okay?"

"Yes. Well, no. I got lost. Didn't you notice?"

He looked sheepish. He'd been dancing. And he figured I would come find him once I was back. So he hadn't been my savior; Jörg, or someone else in the group, had been the one to realize I was missing. But I didn't have the energy to point that out. I was above ground again, there was no need to go into what had happened below, so after a few minutes I got another drink and, despite the ache in my thigh, I followed the example of the other subterranean tourists and slipped back into the fun.

I fell asleep shortly after returning home but woke up two hours later with the makings of a hangover, my sleep driven out by the familiar headache and nausea. Without turning on a light, I stumbled over to the bathroom cabinet, found the bottle of aspirin, and washed down two, perhaps three tablets with a glass of tap water. I got back into bed, stacking up the pillows to lessen the ache, and tried to remember how much I'd drunk at the party. All that came to mind was the bottle of vodka with the generic label and the flimsy plastic glasses and the damp walls of the bowling alley and the way my thigh contin- ued to sting as I said good-bye to Jonas, and my usual reac- tion, just as the night bus was pulling up, which was to lean back as soon as he leaned forward, avoiding, just in time, his expectant mouth.

The following Monday at work I inserted a new tape into the dictaphone and pressed *Play*. The subject of the day's lecture was an abandoned amusement park in Treptow, otherwise known as the Kulturpark Plänterwald, lifespan 1969 to 1989. Yet another closed and crumbling landmark of the former

GDR, this one a stone's throw from the river Spree. Like the television tower (his first mention), this theme park was, according to Weiss, a source of pride for its citizens. With its thirty-six-seat gondola, forty-five-meter-high Ferris wheel, it had been a dazzling attraction, boasting a good 1.7 million visitors a year.

Just as I was beginning to put aside the troubling memory of Saturday night and enter into more neutral territory, that is, the fate of this rusting amusement park with its overgrown vegetation, capsized dinosaurs and stranded Viking boat, Doktor Weiss's voice decided to withdraw. I'd begun transcribing a passage on the Ferris wheel when something, presumably, jammed, and, as if suddenly plunged underwater, the historian's trim, elegant voice slowed to a demonic slur. Treptower Park became Treeeeeptooooowwweerr Paaaark. Spree became Sppreeee. Vowels deepened, consonants stretched, and everything dropped an octave or two while the words themselves emerged farther and farther apart. After a few minutes there was no word to follow the last and the long stream I was so used to hearing had crystallized into something like a frozen waterfall. I opened the dictaphone. A long, shiny spool came cascading out. With the help of a ribbed pencil I managed to reel the tape back in, but when I pressed *Play* I heard nothing. I rewound a bit more, pressed *Play* again. Nothing. Weiss's words had been erased, as if evaporating upon contact with the air. I pressed *Rewind, Fast Forward,* flipped the tape over. I banged the tape on my desk and then against the wall. Nothing. The voice was lost, at least for the day.

I debated what to do. I was loath to knock on Weiss's door and interrupt him at work. On the other hand, perhaps the tape was defective from the start, in which case it was not my fault and he should be notified, and I didn't plan to spend the next three hours sitting at my desk staring at the uncooperative dictaphone.

He took a few minutes to answer and opened the door just a crack. "Yes?"

"The tape . . . it won't play."

He frowned.

"It just . . . I was transcribing and then it just stopped."

In the background I could see Murci pacing back and forth, his tail tucked under and his ears pinned back—lingering in attendance, I couldn't help thinking, like St. Jerome's lion.

"Well, let me have a look." Weiss stepped out of his study and closed the door, leaving the dog inside.

He was wearing a new robe today, this one purple instead of dark blue, I noticed as he sat down at my desk and picked up the dictaphone. He pressed *Play*. Nothing happened. He pressed *Stop*, and then *Play* again. Nothing. I was relieved it hadn't been my imagination. With arthritic hands, a woody swelling around each joint, the historian removed the tape, turned it over, and pressed *Play*. After a few seconds a strangled sound emerged, like a sunken object gurgling back up to the surface. It gurgled for a few seconds and then went dead. Weiss opened the dictaphone and removed the tape.

"It's probably defective. That's bad news, unless I remember all I said . . . Can you recall what was on it?"

"You were talking about the amusement park."

"What about it?"

"Its Ferris wheel."

"Oh yes, the Ferris wheel in Plänterwald. And what else?"

I tried to remember the words I'd heard slowing down, the names that had lost their momentum and sunk underwater, but for some reason nothing came back.

"Do you remember anything else?" Doktor Weiss asked as he continued to press buttons and fiddle with the tape. All the pressing and fiddling made me nervous. I had the feeling that at any moment the device might break and I'd be out of a job, but I just sat and stared with growing yet unspoken concern, like the time I sat by my sister Yvonne while she prepared dinner with her long, fuchsia fingernails, waiting for a nail to chip into the vegetables she was chopping with vigor but instead of saying anything I had just sat there and watched until the inevitable happened, and when I drew her attention to the flakes of polish amidst the carrots she flew into a rage and banished me from the kitchen.

I will never be able to explain why, but after a few minutes I broke down. It might have been the sight of the old historian in his purple robe fussing with the dictaphone, searching for his own voice, or my fear of losing the job should anything go wrong, or the sudden stark futility of his endeavor, and mine, and everyone else's; whatever the cause, I found myself sobbing.

His frown dissolved as he set down the dictaphone. "What's wrong?"

I bit my hand to force myself to stop crying, an unbecoming indulgence I'd always tried to avoid, especially in public. When I was growing up my sisters cried at the drop of a hat and my mother at every parting, even from a second cousin she had met once in her life, yet like the shutter to the semicircle I found it just as mysterious, this connection between sadness and salty liquid.

Weiss extracted a handkerchief from his robe and offered it to me.

"What's wrong?" he repeated, laying a tentative hand on my shoulder.

I debated whether to tell him.

"Tatiana?" He withdrew his hand.

Once again I buckled, giving him all the details, omitting nothing except that I'd been invited to the party by Jonas Krantz.

He was less surprised than I'd expected him to be. Indeed, he didn't seem surprised at all. It was almost as if he had been down there with me and I were recounting something he knew well, firsthand. He listened attentively, however, and when I was finished with my account, nearly breaking into a sweat at the memory of those oozing walls, Weiss said, "Well, yes. Nothing ever vanishes."

I asked whether he thought the bowling alley would have been Nazi or Stasi.

He paused. "What was the address of this post office?"

"Somewhere on Krausenstraße."

"I'm almost certain it would have been used by the Stasi, but we can look into it. Perhaps I should send you back there to take a few notes. Maybe some pictures too."

"I'll never go back down. From now on I will try to avoid underground spaces as much as possible."

"It's not just spaces below," Weiss said, before bringing up "the brick demon of the Wasserturm" again, as well as examples of top floors and other "upper regions" that creaked under the burden of their past, and while he spoke my thoughts drifted, for the first time ever in the presence of my employer, and as he reeled off more examples of "problematic" places in Berlin and Brandenburg, not to mention Munich, with such ease it seemed he'd prepared the day's lecture in advance, I realized what I had to do when I returned home that afternoon.

*   *   *

Inside the building, the stairs lay grey and quiet like rows of sleeping pigeons and as I walked past my apartment and on to the next flight it occurred to me that I'd never given these stairs, or the stairwell, much thought. I paused at the landing, this intermediate place between my territory and the unknown, a flat horizontal surface interrupting the smooth flow of stairs. Most people, I reckoned, paid no attention to landings, enforced pauses between two vertical distances, concerning themselves only with the stairs and where they led. Like most stairwells this one was U-shaped, and I had to make a 180-degree turn before continuing past my floor and ascending, step by step, into foreign terrain.

Two large padlocks hung on the door, two detachable mouths, firmly shut. One was copper, the other painted blue. I knocked, though I knew there could be no answer, then knocked again. I tried forcing the door but the locks remained in place as if obeying a past command. I pulled a bobby pin from my hair and tested my dexterity. A jiggle to the left, a jiggle to the right, up and down and sideways, and then, all of a sudden, a click and the first lock yielded. Ditto the second. Having never picked a lock in my life, I felt encouraged and pushed the door open.

I entered slowly. After all, I didn't want to startle anyone, especially someone given to such seclusion. What if I came face-to-face with the moon-driven merchant or the restless Goth in the midst of one of his activities? I hadn't even thought up something to say to explain my presence. I held my breath and stepped in as quietly as I could, like Bluebeard's final wife entering the forbidden attic, aware that from now on my actions would be irreversible.

I could describe the room in a number of ways. I could focus on how the afternoon light entered in slanted columns through the windows, or the way the stuccoed walls offered up an infinite number of patterns. I could mention the curious juxtaposition of the furniture—a wooden stool, a three-legged table and a tiled coal oven filled with unburned lumps of coal—or the overall play of shapes, a giant-sized jigsaw puzzle with a few missing pieces. I could describe the distant murmur of the street, the way the silence was occasionally punctuated, as I stood there, by an insistent car horn. I could focus on the wooden floors, how each floorboard was distinct from its neighbor, marked with its own set of slits and grooves. I could mention the sense of vacancy, pervasive unless one took into account the particles of dust that circulated in the unbreathed air and coated the ground so thickly my shoes left their print, or the tiny corner bathroom with its two windows sealed with insulating tape, or the grimy knobs and sticky faucets.

But what drew my attention most was a greyish outline on one of the walls, several degrees darker than the surrounding white. It was clearly a place where a picture had once hung. From the moment I saw it, this empty square unnerved me. I stood staring at it, unable to pull myself away until the car horn broke my train of thought and put an end to my contemplation, which resumed seconds later when I turned back to the square, and I thought about the scores I'd erased from the wall in the bowling alley, wondering what had been left on the wall, probably a white smudge of chalk, after I'd rubbed them with my fist, and wondering whether this dark imprint was somehow mocking me, reminding me of the inevitable, which was, of course, that nothing can truly be rubbed away or blotted out, and how the more you try to rub something away the darker it becomes.

Before leaving I wandered through the rooms a second time, running my hands over every surface until they were black, searching, almost hoping, for a sign of life. I couldn't help sensing that this apartment possessed a memory of everything the building had ever witnessed, every voice and step and desire of its former inhabitants, stored up and filed in one vast archive. The noises I heard at night were probably vestigial sounds from decades past, footfalls made by shoes never reclaimed. That's what Doktor Weiss would have said, anyhow.

But it was the grey outline on the wall, more than any restless memory at night, that unsettled me, and when I finally tore my gaze from it, I saw squares dancing before my eyes. I hurried out and rehung the locks, mouths given something new to chew, then took the stairs two at a time and once home I splashed cold water over my face until the squares disappeared from inside my lids. I never told Weiss about my visit upstairs, but after I went up there the sounds began to subside, as if deactivated.

The days grew colder. The furniture shop near my house closed down, replaced, a few weeks later, by a small boutique selling outlandish hats. The NPD won seats in Saxony and Mecklenburg–Western Pomerania. Weiss worried about that, and about Murci, who wasn't eating well. The noises upstairs continued to subside and I found it easier to fall asleep at night, though cracks of light still shone in through the curtains and I had begun using a sleeping mask again. The sound machine remained wrapped in a plastic bag at the back of my closet. Every now and then I thought of calling Jonas Krantz but would hang up halfway through dialing.

Once the November chill set in the words of the real estate agent returned to haunt me. *There's no central heating,* she had said, *or radiators. Only a coal oven that needs to be cleaned, professionally cleaned.* This lowered the rent so I accepted. After all, I'd thought at the time, I knew my Berlin autumns and winters; no one need tell me how to keep myself warm. After five years abroad I was not the kind of Mexican who expected the sun to follow her halfway around the globe, but as the days grew colder my home felt less and less welcoming and one morning I woke up to find a thin layer of ice on the glass of water by my bed. I tapped it with a pen, remembering one unusually cold winter in Matepec when the village shoemaker had to suspend work since his pot of glue had frozen. Still, the cold was nowhere as bad as during my first German winter, when the temperature dropped to minus twenty-five and the zoo had to move its penguins indoors; admission was half price since so many of the animals had been brought inside or remained in hibernation longer than usual.

It wasn't any cozier at work. Weiss too must have been trying to save money on heating. He began to wear a black turtleneck under his purple robe and Murci was bundled up in a knit sweater, both shielded against the drafts that swept through their ground-floor apartment. Mornings when I arrived the dictaphone and computer keys, not yet warmed by my fingertips, were ice cold, and I would rarely remove my coat, this coat I wore most seasons, as I sat transcribing.

Time seemed to be slowing down. The hours dragged by with enormous reluctance. Aside from my excursions to Charlottenburg, every day weighed more or less the same. There were, however, a few signs that time had passed, apart from the shift in season: an addition upstairs (a young accountant named Felix moved into the empty apartment) and a subtraction downstairs (one of the old ladies passed away). I only knew of the latter because for a few days a steady stream of mourners entered the building, visitors with white hair and black suits, shrunken men carrying bunches of chrysanthemums twice their size. Who would have imagined my neighbors were acquainted with so many people? I did not know which of the ladies had died; despite my encounter with Frau Heller their faces constituted one ravaged amalgam, but since the death the other two stopped observing me from their window.

One afternoon, to my surprise, Doktor Weiss asked me to conduct another interview. This time I was to choose the subject myself.

"Find someone who in some way embodies the city for you," he said. "Can you think of someone?"

"Yes," I answered immediately.

"Well, think of ways in which this person can illuminate their corner of the city. Think of things that only he or she would be able to describe. The more specific, the better."

There was no doubt whom I would interview. I waited until the next day of clement weather—we'd had a spell of crystalline skies but piercingly chilly afternoons—and alighted from the tram at Alexanderplatz, now the site of one of the dozens of Christmas markets that had recently appeared across the city. Starting in late November these markets would spring up in every square and empty lot, and here, to accompany the competing stands of gluhwein, sausages and kitschy carved ornaments, an ice rink blasting disco music had been set up in front of the department store. The last of the cranes had been carted off, clearing the space for something even less scenic, I was sorry to see, for the rink was not only a repugnant sight, dozens of red-nosed kids elbowing ahead of one other, shoving and screaming and falling on their rumps, but with its loud, tinny music it was also an assault on the ears, turning the entire square into a cheap amusement park.

As ever, the Simpleton didn't seem to take notice. There she stood, near the Deutsche Bank cash machines, oblivious to the commotion across the street. That day she had three, no, four, plastic bags strung over her left arm and a bare branch in her right hand. She wasn't wearing gloves and her skin was a bluish white, as if developing its own inner layer of frost.

I felt shy but determined, a sense of duty propelling me forwards. My black leather boots approached her blue plastic slippers. Soon they would be face-to-face. I had seen the woman so many times that I couldn't help feeling, just slightly, that I knew her.

The moment she saw me she transferred the branch to her left hand and stretched out her right, and opened it, smiling her sweet, village-idiot smile.

"Good afternoon," I said.

She continued to smile and looked down at her hand, calling my attention to the empty palm. I placed four euros in it. She mumbled something and counted the coins, her eyes widening when she grasped the amount.

"Good afternoon," I repeated, and then asked, gently, "would you mind if I asked you a few questions?"

She studied me, my coat, my boots, my face.

"It'll only take a few minutes."

"Okay," she said quietly.

I hadn't written down my questions but had gone through them in my head, assuming she would respond more easily if I weren't holding a pen and paper. The answers would have to be memorized and then quickly written down once we'd parted ways.

"Where are you from?"

The Simpleton smiled.

"Are you from Berlin?"

She giggled like a child.

"Are you from Germany?"

She giggled again, this time covering her mouth. Her fingers were long and elegant, her nails full of grime.

"What's your name?"

She held up her hand and pointed three fingers downward to form an M.

"Does your name start with M?"

"Mmhmm."

"Is your name Marie?"

The Simpleton giggled even more and shook her head.

"Masha?"

She shook her head again.

"Margarethe?"

"No!" she shrieked, laughing. I decided to move on to the next question; we could return to the matter of her name later.

"How long have you been coming here, to this spot?"

She uttered her first phrase. "A long time."

"How long?"

She scrunched up her face to think. The smile vanished. Everything became contorted, lost in a mass of indecision. There was nothing like an indecisive face, I realized, a face whose features, from one second to the next, lose their focus. A makeshift expression, in which the scaffolding of serious deliberation props everything up for a few seconds before letting it lapse back into the sea of another smile. The Simpleton's face did this each time I asked a challenging question.

"How long, then?"

"A long time."

"Tell me," I said softly.

She looked into my eyes and said, "I have stood here on 118 windy afternoons, 26 days of sun, 94 evenings of drizzle and 102 mornings so cold my toes almost froze off."

"So in total . . . ?" Weiss would want precise answers.

She paused to think. The smile receded.

"I have seen 121 tourists walk past with guidebooks, 169 dogs, most of them on leashes, one wheezing cat, 145 students on secondhand bicycles, 32 skinheads and 14 people in wheelchairs, 9 of them women."

"That sounds like a long time."

She nodded.

"And how many trams have passed?"

"A thousand!" she exclaimed. "A thousand trams a day!"

"And how many cranes have you seen this past year?"

She gazed up into the sky, then scratched the palm of her hand, which was now empty. The coins I'd given her must have been slipped into her pocket when I wasn't looking.

No answer. I returned to more personal questions. "Do you remember the day you started coming here?"

"Yes! It was a Tuesday morning. I ate a bowl of muesli and washed my hair in the sink. Or maybe I washed my hair and then ate the muesli. A few hours later I was hungry again. And the bread at the station bakery always smells so good!"

"Can you remember which Tuesday that was?"

"Yes! It was the Tuesday after the Monday on which I ate bread with jam since I'd run out of muesli. But then I walked to Aldi and bought a half-kilo bag. I didn't wash my hair that day but it didn't matter since it rained on my way home."

"Can you remember anything else from that day?"

"Yes! It was the day I saw the man with the poodle. The poodle was wearing a woolen sweater. It was also the day the bus driver shouted at me because I took a long time counting my change and there were people behind me waiting to get on the bus."

"Do you remember the season?"

She shook her head.

"But you say the poodle was wearing a sweater? Perhaps it was winter?"

"Yes, the poodle was wearing a sweater. It was a blue and purple sweater and it didn't match the color of its fur. Maybe it wasn't a poodle."

"And do you remember what you were wearing?"

She paused to think.

"A flowered dress. A dress with flowers on it. Material cut into a triangle with a flower pattern. I have many flowered dresses. In fact, all my dresses have flowers. I love flowers, especially on dresses."

"And how many hours do you stand here every day?"

The Simpleton smiled, once more armed with an answer and eager to respond.

"When I arrive in the morning my socks are white and when I go home in the evening they are grey. When I arrive in the morning I am full from breakfast but when I go home in the evening my stomach is grumbling. When I arrive in the morning the hair inside my scarf smells nice but when I go home in the evening it smells dirty, like city. That's how many hours."

"Are you hungry now?"

"No."

"Are you sure? I could go across and buy something at the Christmas market."

"Whenever I see people eating apples I want a banana. And when I see people with lollipops I crave cabbage."

"I see."

"And when I see people in wheelchairs I also see a wheezing cat."

I wasn't sure where to go from there, there must have been some logic that escaped me, and decided to change the subject.

"Don't your feet get cold in winter?"

She wiggled her toes, which emerged awkwardly from the plastic slippers, and shook her head. I thought of another question.

"Do you live far from here?"

She scrunched up her face again, then relaxed it back into a smile. "It is 17 minutes from my house to the bus stop, six minutes by bus to the Ring S-Bahn, 38 minutes on the S-Bahn and 16 minutes on the tram to here."

"That sounds far away."

She pulled a crumpled tissue from a pocket in her dress and wiped her left eye. All of a sudden I worried that my persistent interrogation had made her cry.

"What's wrong?" I asked.

"A midge."

"A midge?"

"A midge flew into my eye."

"From where?"

"I don't know. She was on her way to the store. To do some shopping. She didn't wait for directions. She just kept flying. In the wrong direction. Into my eye."

"Would you like a mirror?"

"No, a wheezing cat."

"I beg your pardon?"

The Simpleton's eyes grew larger. And larger. And then she began to laugh. She tilted her head back, opened her mouth like a donkey and laughed. Her lips whitened and I could count at least six fillings in her teeth. And as she laughed, the laugh became louder and crueler, annulling the vulnerable, childlike aura from earlier. The laugh entered my ears and hit me in the stomach as if someone had taken a good punch. I looked around to see if anyone at the cash machines had noticed the unpleasant peals but at that moment there was no one nearby.

"Well, I won't trouble you any further," I said.

The Simpleton was now *roaring*; her laugh had escalated to a roar, her head thrown back and the fillings in her teeth glinted like the metallic sphere of the television tower. Without further hesitation I left her and crossed the street in the direction of Alexanderplatz and its Christmas festivities, which now seemed so well-wishing and innocuous. After the Simpleton's demonic, yes, demonic, laugh, this red and white and green striped ruckus was music to my ears, the tinny disco sounds overlaying the grotesque soundtrack I'd just heard.

That night as I lay in bed with my sleeping mask on I could still hear her laughing from her spot near the Deutsche Bank cash machines, a deep, throaty laugh aimed directly at me, the village idiot from Mexico who actually thought she knew Berlin and its inhabitants well enough to go up and demand answers to mindless questions only a tourist would ask.

In addition to the Christmas markets, winter made itself felt in other ways. Marzipan bears with raisin eyes winked from the windows of my bakery. The trams filled with bronchial coughs and sneezes programmed to erupt just as the name of each stop was announced. In anticipation of the early dusk the streetlights hummed on at ten past four. Some people put up a fight and clung to their autumn wardrobe, but for the most part there was a proliferation of hats and coats and gloves.

On the night of our second "date" Jonas Krantz wore jeans and a black cap angled slightly to the left. After a few weeks' deliberation I had called him. He suggested meeting at a bar off Friedrichstraße, one with leather sofas and orangey lights, a far cry from the post office party, but perhaps he chose it for that very reason. To reach the bar I got off the bus a few stops before Potsdamer Platz, a real eyesore as far as I was concerned, a futuristic playground built from scratch in the late nineties. Nearby was the Sony Center complex with its loud American thunder and soaring buildings like curved, shiny razor blades. And then there was the Philharmonic, which, depending on the time of day, resembled a thatched basket with a peaked lid or a bizarre, honeycombed pastry, and a few steps up from the Philharmonic lay the Gemäldegalerie with its sterile facade and sloping walkways on which skateboarders practiced in summer, deceptive Berlin places where the sublimity of the interior wasn't quite matched by the awkward geometry of the exterior.

Over shots of tequila Jonas told me about his father, a large man who once crushed a kitten in his sleep. But what could he do, Herr Krantz had insisted the next morning as he laid the flattened corpse on the kitchen table, when in his sleep he'd merely rolled over onto this thing that had been too small and weak to protest? That's the sort of man my father was, Jonas said, and ordered another shot of tequila with two slices of lemon, at my suggestion, on the side. He showed no remorse and by afternoon seemed to have forgotten about the incident though his children thought about it for years to come and attributed all kinds of blockages to that vision of the flattened kitten amidst the breakfast plates.

Unable to dredge up an equivalent memory (there must have been at least a few I was forgetting), I told him instead about D'Rodrigo, the neighborhood beauty salon two doors down from our deli in Polanco, where we seemed to spend an inordinate amount of time. You could almost say it was our third home, this cramped rectangular room with three swivel chairs and one long, cloudy mirror. Whenever I needed a trim I would get it from Rodrigo himself, a toupeed man in his fifties, and each time he cut my hair slightly differently. It didn't always work, but I rarely cared unless there was someone of interest at school.

Haircuts were administered on the swivel chair over-looked by a shelf holding eleven Styrofoam heads, each with a note pinned to the neck. Sometimes these heads had wigs on them and sometimes they were bald, revealing pockmarks and deformities in the skull. At first I thought Rodrigo's salon doubled as a successful wig shop until one day, overcome by curiosity, I climbed onto a small bench and read the notes. Each slip of paper bore a different name (Sharon, Deborah, Mónica), telephone number and set of instructions (part on the left, add highlights, wash and detangle), and it didn't take long to deduce that these wigs, on permanent rotation, be-longed to Hasidic women, many of them our customers too, who would drop them off periodically for styling.

One of the few gentiles who spent time at D'Rodrigo, apart from Rodrigo himself and his troupe of lady assistants, was an old man who would get his nails done every afternoon while his wife shopped at the market around the corner. He was obsessive about the state of his hands and rumor had it he refused to accompany his wife on her errands lest he should be asked to carry something heavy and tear a nail. Every now and then I too would get a manicure, on days when I had to wait longer than usual for my parents to close the shop. I would sit at a low table across from a gum-smacking woman with copper hair and gaze down at my nails, ten little shovels painted the color of tubercular blood. The pleasure began a few days later when the varnish started to chip away, the top rim first and then, depending on my activities of the week, the rest of the coat would go, unevenly. You would only notice the erosion if my hands were at rest, otherwise the nails still looked elegant, a harmonious blur, just like the days themselves, which passed without consequence unless you pinned one down and examined it too closely.

The tequila rose to our heads—I realized I'd been chattering on and on, about insignificant things compared to what Jonas had just told me—and my eyes began to sting from the bar's thickening curtain of cigarette smoke, to which we contributed with some Russian cigarettes he had brought along. A bit more smoke, another coat on the lungs, what did one night matter, I thought to myself, especially since everything else about the evening was out of the ordinary, beginning with my having picked up the phone and called a man, something I hadn't done in years.

"Let's go somewhere else," he said at around midnight.

The moon was nearly full that night, and because it was nearly full there was only one place, Jonas said, one place we had to visit.

We walked down Unter den Linden, the trees atwinkle with white holiday lights, and past the regally lit Brandenburg Gate, a different creature from that evening in 1986, then turned left before arriving at a sea of upright concrete slabs, which I recognized immediately as the new Holocaust memorial. I had yet to visit the place but had read about the controversy surrounding it, some people saying it was too vulnerable and exposed, others complaining it was only dedicated to the murdered Jews and not to other victims of the Nazis, others criticizing the barrenness of the place and its lack of so-called aesthetic principles, and yet others said it was *too* aestheticized and didactic. Each time there was a new memorial voices of all tenors would start clamoring, always in disagreement, even about whether these monuments were necessary in the first place.

Once inside the new memorial, the space, which at first seemed so open and exposed, closed in on us with each step we took, the 2711 concrete slabs like a stalled army converging from all sides. Despite the hundreds of possible exits and entrances it was hard not to feel an immediate wave of claustrophobia and disorientation, and wherever I looked I saw dark pillars, some only half a meter high, others looming overhead. The sloping ground made it hard to secure a foothold and every few meters I found myself grabbing onto the slabs to steady myself, although I had the feeling that at any moment they might treacherously tilt away. It was the topography of the place that threw me off balance, not the tequila from the bar, and before long everything was undulating and vertiginous and the only steady presence was the moon, whose beams washed the stones, skimmed the tops and dissolved.

The plinths seemed to lean in a million directions as I followed Jonas, keeping an eye on his black cap lest the rest of him disappear. I couldn't even fathom whether our movements were upward or downward since the ground robbed me of any surety. It was like walking among 2711 upended sarcophagi, 2711 souls awaiting judgment, in an ad hoc graveyard devoid of markings or inscriptions.

Soon we were at its center.

"Let's play hide and seek," Jonas said.

"Are you joking?"

"Please."

"But what if we lose each other?" Wherever I turned I saw processions of grey, endless grey unfolding into more grey.

"We won't."

"We will. It's dark."

"There's the moon. And our voices. We can always call out to each other."

"But . . ."

"But what?"

I was trying to find a good excuse, something other than the truth, which was that I was terrified of getting lost in that forest of monoliths. But before I knew it Jonas had disappeared.

"Go on, find me!" he called out.

I walked towards where his voice had come from.

"This way!" I heard him call from another direction.

I turned ninety degrees but all I met with was the same sea of slabs, as speechless as the night, while the moon gazed down, poetically but uselessly, from above, and as I gazed back up at the moon I decided I was not going to go along with Jonas's game.

"I'm sorry, I can't do this," I called out, taking a few steps towards where I hoped an exit might be found.

"Jonas?"

No response.

"Jonas? I don't want to play anymore. Let's go."

The site held fast to its silence, not a sound was heard apart from the distant drone of traffic, and, contrary to what Jonas had assured me, I felt it had robbed us of our voices. In their variety of heights, the slabs were like a horizon of unfinished sentences, each truncated at a different moment, nothing but aborted utterances.

"Jonas?" His name sank amidst the stones and was lost.

I continued taking small steps in the direction of the traffic sounds, or in what I thought was the direction of the traffic, but after a few minutes I realized I wasn't getting anywhere and it occurred to me to climb onto one of the smaller steles to have a look around. Just as I was lifting my foot someone grabbed me from behind and covered my eyes with two rough hands. I felt heavy male breathing in my ear as the hands pressed harder against my eyes, and I tried to break free but it was no use, although I had nothing to fear since it was Jonas, of course, breathless from his exertions to find me, Jonas, who kissed me on the neck with cold lips, and this time I let him, although his lips were as cold as the stone slabs and without the antigraffiti varnish not half as smooth.

From afar his purple robe looked regal but from up close I could see threads unraveling, the hem dragging and a button missing from the sleeve, and I couldn't tell whether it was actually made of silk or of some sort of rayon pretending to be silk. Weiss always wore his robes wrapped tight, as if mortally afraid of drafts or other menacing intruders that might find their way in. Contrary to what I first thought, it did not fit him perfectly and there was a certain snugness around the chest and shoulders that seemed to restrict movement, something I only noticed when he walked into my room and held up a sheet of paper, the sleeve of his robe inching its way down and the fabric across the chest growing tauter.

"What is this?" he asked, waving the paper.

"What's what?"

"This thing about the Simpleton of Alexanderplatz."

He did not seem amused, interested, or in the least bit grateful, though I had transcribed all her answers, omitting nothing but the final demonic laugh.

"It's the interview I conducted. I thought you would . . . like it."

He stared at me for a few seconds before coming over to my desk. "Who is this person? Does she really exist?"

"It's a woman I often see near the tram stop at Alexanderplatz."

"And the midge? What is the midge supposed to represent?"

"I . . . it was something she was telling me. A midge flew into her eye towards the end of the interview."

"And the wheezing cat? Did you see any wheezing cat?"

"No. That's something she mentioned. I didn't see one."

"Tatiana, I hope you don't mind my asking, but is everything all right?"

"Yes."

"Are you happy in Berlin?"

"Yes."

"Do you have friends?"

"Sometimes."

"A partner?"

"Sometimes."

"Do you enjoy this job?"

"Very much."

"I'm just a little puzzled. It's not your fault. You had no training for this job. And your transcriptions are very good. You should be proud of your work. My only request is that you stay on track."

"I will."

"So forget what I said last time. No more interviews for now. Let's stick to the transcriptions."

* * *

After the bungled interview I dreaded passing the Deutsche Bank cash machines but it turned out I had nothing to fear, for the next time the tram went by the Simpleton wasn't there, nor the next, nor the next, regardless of whether I was on my way to work or coming home in the late afternoon. After a week or two I came to the conclusion that she had either grown tired of the spot and chosen another street corner, or else had been flustered by my interview and decided to move elsewhere, but either way, Alexanderplatz lost its smile, or at least what had seemed like a smile although now, looking back, there had been something sinister dancing around that smile, a slightly derisory curling of the lips, a scarcely perceptible undertow that sullied the benevolence I thought to have glimpsed so many times from the window of the tram.

I still had so much time on my hands, too much time, and yet I found it as hard as ever to account for all the hours in Berlin which passed like minutes or even seconds, unable to hold onto time, water in a sieve. Often I would sit for what seemed like eternal stretches at the kitchen table and eat bread and honey. German bread was one of the main attractions of living in the country and after five years I had tried all the varieties I could find, starting with pumpernickel and sourdough but soon moving on to every possible combination of salt, yeast, flour and water, and as for honey, well, a love of honey ran in the family; one of my grandfathers was a beekeeper and had an apiary in Matepec, and we sold eight flavors of honey at the deli.

When I wasn't eating bread and honey I still went for my walks, although I found it hard to clear my head with so many people around. Cities were so much about sound and motion, and on some days I simply had no desire to cross paths with anyone, not even strangers on the street, so like the disfigured person who only leaves his house after dusk I would wait until it grew dark to go out and then keep to the quieter streets, and as I walked I would look up, every few meters, in search of that illusion of the moon traveling across the heavens while the clouds try in vain to keep up, a temptress in perpetual flight from her flock of suitors.

Apart from snacking and walks I found a few other ways of killing time, some more productive than others. For instance, I became a member of the Dark Skies Association. The slivers of light coming through my curtains had yet to wane, and they so vexed me that I joined this noble association, which for only twenty euros a year promised monthly newsletters packed with advice, an elegant membership certificate and a sleeping mask made of Egyptian cotton. It was a serious matter, this relentlessly lit world of ours that is never turned off, and the more I focused on the light entering my room at every ungodly hour and the processions of streetlamps that threw things out of kilter by diluting the ascendancy of the moon, the more imperative it became to join this association which strove to preserve darkness in cities and in the countryside, a cause I have endorsed ever since one night in my early adolescence.

It had been chilly for September, I recall, and my mother, sisters and I huddled in our shawls counting the minutes until eleven while my father and brothers paced back and forth nearby. That year, as every other, we had traveled to Matepec, the verdant, imperturbable village where my father had grown up, eight hours by car from Mexico City, to celebrate the day in September 1810 when Father Miguel Hidalgo rang the church bells in the town of Dolores and called for an end to nearly three centuries of Spanish rule.

The village square was swarming with locals and visitors from neighboring villages who preferred the Grito of Matepec to their own festivities. Smoking cigarettes and swilling pulque, a group of mariachis lounged under an ancient ash tree. A ring of spotlights had been positioned to shine onto the bandstand at the center of the square, turning it into something like a flying saucer, and before long the mayor would hold court from its platform, delivering the famous cry of Independence that every Mexican knows from the age of two. The spotlights were echoed by hundreds of smaller lights, tucked into flower beds and strung from every pole and streetlamp, and you could hardly tell whether it was day or night.

At five to eleven a coiffed, tubby man with a mustache and cream-colored suit, the recently elected mayor of Matepec, mounted the bandstand to a gleeful fanfare of mariachi trumpets and violins. The throng pressed closer and above the cheers some of the more soused spectators began to hoot, loud and triumphant, as if their independence had been won that very evening. The mayor grinned into the lights, a self-satisfied donkey, and took the flag from Matepec's sole policeman.

The hour arrived, the bells from the church pealed once. The mayor's smile took over his face and he opened his mouth wide, drawing in enough air to impart a long, vibrant Grito, and exhaled, "*Viva . . .*"

But his cry was cut short by a loud squawking, or perhaps it was halfway between a squawking and a cawing, that suddenly invaded the square. Crossing the heavily illuminated night was an arrow-shaped formation of long-legged birds, probably cranes, hundreds of them. To everyone's surprise, they did not fly over and away, but began to circle the square, once, twice, three times. The mayor dropped the flag; the mariachis clutched their instruments with uncertainty. All heads turned towards the sky. I too fixed my eyes above, marveling at how the cranes kept to their geometrical formation, not a single bird straying from its allotted place.

"I know what the trouble is," I remember my mother saying, "the clouds are thick tonight and they block out the moon. These birds are confused and are looking for another source of light. Unfortunately, that source happens to be all these crazy lights in the square, which lead them nowhere."

After watching the birds circle for several minutes I turned to look at the mayor, who couldn't hide his exasperation and with increasingly frantic gestures was trying to draw attention back to himself. He crossed his arms and uncrossed them, yawned without covering his mouth, took a step towards the stairs of the bandstand as if considering a retreat. He must have thought better of it though, this squat, mustachioed cream puff, for he returned to his place in the lights. The air was turning colder, the villagers more restless. The big clock on the square read eight minutes past eleven. By now the Grito would have resounded from balconies and bandstands throughout the country, except here in Matepec. Something would have to happen soon. And so the mayor, ignoring the hapless birds, gestured to the mariachis to strike up another tune. The trumpets and violins sang out a second time, although to my ears they sounded far less jubilant.

When the band finished its song the mayor again sucked in his chest, opened his mouth wide, and brayed, "*Mexicanos, ¡vivan los héroes que nos dieron patria!*"

"*¡Viva!*" the villagers roared back.

Above the human cries we heard the cranes squawk, an avian call to arms in response to our own.

"*¡Viva Hidalgo!*"

More cawing overhead.

"*¡Viva!*"

All seven of us remained in the square long after the mayor had been driven off in his black Volkswagen Beetle, long after the mariachis had stowed away their instruments, long after the inebriated villagers, many splattered by the cranes, zigzagged back to their homes or collapsed in maguey fields on the way. We waited until the lights on the poles and in the trees and flowerbeds had been switched off, releasing their grip on the circling birds, and watched as the flock broke out of the aerial loop in which it had been trapped and flew westwards, in the direction of the mountains.

* * *

When it first arrived, I read the newsletter from the Dark Skies Association over and over again, lamenting, together with the hundreds of other members, I imagine, the saturation of light in our modern world and how most people didn't realize that the purpose of darkness was just as important as that of daylight. Man needed to address his fear of the dark rather than find ways of circumventing it. As far as I could remember, apart from my misadventures in the Gestapo bowling alley and the Holocaust memorial I had never been scared of the dark, not even all the times in Mexico when the electricity went out during a storm and I was the only person at home and had to find the candles.

The newsletter mentioned night-migrating birds like the cranes of Matepec that fared far worse in cities, often colliding with buildings and windows and even with each other, plummeting midjourney to the sidewalks below. One officer of the Fatal Light Awareness Program estimated that at least a hundred million birds were killed annually by man-made structures, and that was just birds, forget about turtle hatchlings who crawl suicidally away from the sea towards artificial sky glows and all kinds of insects, especially moths, who fly to their deaths at night. The newsletter was distressing yet I could not keep from reading and rereading it, like a patient newly diagnosed with a disease who can't do anything but research the ailment in every medical journal she can lay her hands on, feeding her panic with ever more detail despite knowing there is little she can do about the problem herself.

I decided to see Jonas Krantz one last time, and by that I meant *the last*. Anything beyond would seem too much like dating. But I also needed to keep functioning on some level outside of my three days at work, before all the little neuroses pooled into something larger, and furthermore, I had a growing ache between my legs that needed attending to by someone other than myself. I'd begun taking long baths in my Soviet tub, lying quietly as I watched the water rise, first above my waist, then closing in on my breasts, circling the nipples until they were covered, and there I'd remain until the water grew cold. Sometimes I wouldn't bother filling the tub and would reach straightaway for the detachable showerhead whose reliable rush of warm water always worked wonders, and by the time it was all over the bathroom mirror was too foggy for me to see myself, a cloudy rectangle that withheld its promise of reflection, and although I enjoyed these moments of small, fleeting ecstasy it would no doubt be pleasant, I reckoned, to have someone else take care of things for once.

There was no hesitation in his voice. He would be at my house within the hour. I took a bath, shaved my legs and rubbed my body with some Dr. Hauschka lavender oil I'd found on sale at the local organic shop.

*   *   *

We didn't linger in the kitchen, just got our beers, bottles that had been chilling in the refrigerator since I'd moved in, and headed to the bedroom, where Jonas sat down a foot away from me on the bed and took a look around, his eyes roaming from the Remedios Varo postcards taped to the walls to the IKEA bookshelves and lopsided closet to the fake Art Nouveau dragonfly lamp.

I told him about the Dark Skies Association. To my surprise, he too was a member, and had been one for years.

"Light pollution. Not good. Electric light did away with the concept of one luminous center. Both at home and in the sky above."

I cast an accusatory glance at the ugly bulb dangling from the ceiling while we sipped at our beers side by side, and then he said, "Can I tell you about something that happened to me last year, something that's been on my mind lately, for some reason, since meeting you?"

"Sure."

My consenting to hear his story seemed to be interpreted as some broader gesture of surrender and without further ado Jonas set down his beer, switched off the light overhead in favor of the dragonfly lamp and moved to the center of the bed, where he embraced me from behind, slipping his arms around my torso. It felt nice, I didn't object, and I listened to him speak without seeing his face, only feeling the vibrations in his chest, against which I let my head fall.

"One day last December, on one of those days when you feel fed up with everything in life and just need to leave, I packed a small bag, left my dog plenty of food and water, and took the train to the Harz Mountains," he said, raising his hands to my breasts and massaging them as he spoke. "Without thinking twice I headed straight for Mount Brocken, which I'd never been to though of course I'd read stories about Walpurgisnacht and the devilish folk living on its upper ridges. You know, *Now to the Brocken the witches ride . . .* Once I got there I climbed and climbed, just me and my bag, through the cold air that got colder and colder, and as I neared the peak, the highest peak of the whole mountain range, something happened: I stopped and looked down, down into a bank of mist—it was probably around five in the afternoon, or actually earlier since in winter the light leaves by four—and as I looked down I saw the shadow of a man, his head surrounded by two concentric iridescent rings," he said, rubbing my breasts harder. "It was my shadow, of course, hovering there below, as if challenging me to a duel. Suddenly my whole existence felt reduced to this, to an illusion on a mountain top, and I began to fear that as soon as the sun withdrew completely— it was already low on the horizon, though it continued to shine—my mind would be blotted out and my body would cease to exist in this fantastical world up on Mount Brocken, all due to the backward scattering of light by individual water droplets."

"Please don't press down so hard."

Jonas barely reduced the pressure. "And when all this was happening, I thought of my life up there on the eighteenth floor of a Plattenbau in Marzahn, and about how many fucking evenings I had stood at the window watching the sunset, trying to read the sky, with my dog at my feet, waiting, just waiting, for some vast, irrefutable sign from nature, for a sign that never came."

Upon finishing his story, or reaching what seemed like the conclusion to his story, Jonas stopped rubbing my breasts and flipped me over. "It was the Brocken Specter, of course," he said, kissing my ears and neck.

"The Brocken Specter?"

"Yes, my shadow, magnified and projected on to the mist below, by the sun behind me. And you know what, Tatiana? Most meteorologists would give their left arm to see this, at least the kinds of meteorologists I know, whose imaginations remain a restless step ahead of scientific observation."

He lifted my shirt, unhooked my brassiere, and sucked my breasts before kissing his way down and parting my legs. He kissed softly and gently and at tantalizing intervals, letting me quiver just a little before resuming the journey, and as I closed my eyes and asked myself why I didn't allow myself these small pleasures more often, I imagined him standing on the mountain, standing there contemplating his reflection on a cloud while the sun dissolved into the horizon.

"Forget about dramatic spectacles or optical toys, the Brocken Specter is one of the greatest illusions ever. And I saw it that evening."

Before entering me he added one last thing, though by then I was only half listening at best. "As you've probably noticed, phantoms are created just as often by the shifting angle of the sun as they are by the human brain."

At first he was gentle, a little too gentle, to the point where I barely felt anything, and I found my thoughts wandering from the bags under his eyes to the blunt nose that brushed against mine to the weather charts on his walls to the dour neighbor in the elevator to the poster with the overgrown grass to the flattened cat amidst the breakfast plates to wondering whether Weiss ever had sex and to where the Simpleton had vanished, to trying, just trying, to focus on *nothing at all*, and just as I began telling myself to stop obsessing and empty my mind, or at least separate what was going on above from what was going on below, Jonas stepped up the momentum, knocking my head against the wall as he thrust me up to a better angle, accidentally slipping out, which was no problem since he jammed his way back in, and this time I could feel all of him, every single inch, not just a hint of something hard but the whole damn thing. It was my first time copulating with such a muscular body, even in Mexico my boyfriends were more angle than mass, but I didn't feel smothered or put off.

That said, by the end, once we attained what we'd each wanted to attain and the ache between my legs had been replaced by a tingling soreness far from unpleasant, I began to long for Jonas to leave. I wanted to be alone again, in my bed with my sheets and pillow, no other body warming the space, no other breathing filling the room. We had spent a nice evening but now it was over and all I wanted was for him to stand up, dress and walk out but instead he just lay there dreamy-eyed, gazing into my face with a self-contented grin, the exact kind of self-contented grin that had made me cringe at times in the past. I closed my eyes and pretended to be on the brink of sleep as if sapped by so much activity, and when that didn't work I lifted my head for a few seconds, long enough to see, thanks to the cracks of light entering from the street, that the clock on my night table announced ten to five. He was not getting the message.

"I don't think I can fall asleep with someone else in my bed," I said.

"I'm not the best sleeper either but I'm willing to give it a try," he smiled.

"No, I don't think that would work."

"Falling asleep together?"

"Exactly."

"All right, I'll go home soon. Besides, I have to walk the dog."

"I thought your dog had died."

"I'm taking care of my neighbor's dog this week."

"Well, it'll have been alone for hours now."

"Yes, I know."

Jonas continued to lie there. The passing minutes grew heavier, the sheets smelled sickeningly of brine. I needed to find my pajamas.

This time I was firmer. "I think you should probably go home and I should sleep alone tonight."

He peeled himself away from me and I watched with half-closed eyes as he slipped on his sleeveless white undershirt and then his sweater. It continued to be a novelty, this broad, masculine body, the sort most women admired, and I studied it one last time while he bent over to pull on his boots.

The light in the hall was still on and I watched his silhouette, now fully dressed, lean over and kiss my forehead.

"I think I'm falling in love with you," he whispered.

"Let's not get ahead of ourselves."

I listened from bed as he fiddled with the lock and opened and closed the door and once I heard his footsteps safely on the stairs, imagining him descending with his ringed glory, I got up and changed the sheets before putting on my pajamas and reaching for my mask.

Apart from walks and newsletters and the occasional kiss, the one other activity that kept me busy outside of work was traveling around the city. My love of the S-Bahn and streetcars had far from diminished and each ride, especially on the S-Bahn, was like a thought-ironing excursion, another fix of local anesthetic, and I tried to go as often as possible. Every now and then I felt unprepared for the announcer's voice, as if he were a real person who was suddenly addressing me, but most of the time I'd take a seat and wait for the words to emerge, finding something extremely comforting about a scripted voice and predictable scenery, about knowing exactly what would come next.

Old and new, logic and impulse, grit and glamour, all blurred into one long thread as the elevated train bisected the city: faceless Plattenbaus—the television tower—the river Spree—the restored facades of the Museumsinsel—the Spree again—the shiny metal capitals of VOLKSBÜHNE—AquaDom, the aquarium of the East—dark green treetops—a vast construction site with cranes, orange diplodocuses grazing on the horizon—more treetops, regularly pruned—we'd leave the East, shoot into the West—rows of neoclassical houses with arched, beckoning portals—parking lots with graffitied walls—the Spree again—cobblestone streets with neatly parked cars—a long greenhouse—somber official buildings—a church—a harbor of parked bicycles—and much, much more that my overburdened eye always failed to register.

And then there were the streetcars, yellow caterpillars by day, articulated light boxes by night, that with quiet strength accordioned their way through the East in tiny processions. My new favorite spot was a little alley behind Hackescher Markt where the trams would nap for ten minutes in rows of three, as still as chrysalises, awaiting their next round. As if obeying some universal cliché, each driver would switch off his motor and step out for a cigarette, the white plume of smoke streaking the darkness. It was a peaceful spot, hidden behind the bustle of the busy junction, and I visited it often that winter, finding something soothing, almost human, about large machines at rest.

And then something happened, one night on a tram, which made me question what kind of spaces these streetcars really were. I'd been on my way home from buying a bottle of aspirin at the twenty-four hour pharmacy in Friedrichstraße, arming myself for what I feared might be a migraine. So far it was only an increased sensitivity to light and a pianissimo throbbing at the temples, but I knew from experience what might lie in store. At Alexanderplatz I got off the S-Bahn and walked over to the tram shelter. The circular world clock outside the station had just struck midnight, the television tower, illuminated like a long-necked queen from below. All the seats at the shelter were occupied and I searched for a windproof spot to wait for the M4 tram. The night was chilly and all I had on was a sweater and my habitual coat, weak ammunition against December. A young couple with cans of beer shared a set of headphones to the left of a melancholic fat man in a blue tracksuit whose swollen, amphibian eyes and plump lips seemed to provide an extra buffer between himself and the world. So far it was the usual night, with a pigeoned wind that carried with it the scent of city.

A woman, no, a man, in a red cape walked up. He had shoulder-length graying hair, a pronounced stoop, and thick bangs curled under. His eyebrows were finely brushed and his face was heavy with makeup, yet the effect was oddly discreet. My first guess was that he was an actor too lazy or impatient to change out of his costume after the show, but another glance at the shiny black handbag and Mary Janes supported my second guess, that he was a transvestite. Like his face, his attire had a prim air, almost demure, far from glitzy or seedy. His black skirt fell to below the knee, leaving visible a pair of chunky calves in skin-color tights.

All heads turned in his direction. The red cape must have been a constant attention-grabber yet the transvestite huddled at one end of the shelter, a meter or so from where I was standing, ignoring the collective stare. At one point he coughed, a husky cough, more male than female. The couple with headphones giggled. The melancholic fat man seemed oblivious.

A few minutes later the M4 arrived. Everyone clambered on. I felt a tropism toward the red cape, or perhaps I just wanted to get a closer look, so I waited until the transvestite found a seat and then took one diagonally behind him. He crossed his legs, adjusted his skirt, which had hiked up a little, and smoothed out his collar. I then watched as he pulled a pocket-sized address book out of his purse and began flipping through pages and pages of blue ink, too fast for me to read anything. The tram marched on to the next stop. A few more people boarded. Someone cursed loudly at the ticket machine, accusing it of gobbling down his change. The man in the red cape turned around sharply to see who had interrupted the peace, and as he did I got a good look at his profile, brought into fine definition under the harsh light of the tram. I thought, wait, no, it couldn't be, but it was, or was it my imagination? Beneath the careful makeup and the old-fashioned garb I thought I recognized—and it wasn't the effect of the migraine which had yet to set in—the bosky eyebrows, brushed down but beginning to protest, the thick shock of hair escaping from the neat row of bangs overhead, and the stoop. I tried to picture Weiss in a red cape, adding a few brushstrokes of makeup to his face. Yes, it was him.

I stared at the back of the transvestite's head, willing him to turn around again, but he didn't. Should I tap him on the shoulder and say hello or would he be horrified at our encounter? And what if it was not Weiss but some cranky old queen who simply bore a strong resemblance to my employer? The tram pulled up to the next stop. The caped man turned towards the window and gazed out. He'd put away his address book. I was tempted, extremely tempted, to lean forwards and tap him on the shoulder. But each time I began to seriously consider doing so I held back.

My stop arrived. I rose, reluctantly, from my seat. A strong part of me longed to stay on the tram and follow the transvestite to his destination but all I did was go and stand at the exit in front of him and try to make myself noticed by clearing my throat and then raising an arm to tuck a lock of hair behind my ear. I sensed eyes watching me but couldn't be certain. The tram came to a halt and I stepped out. My feet touched the pavement, the doors closed. A painted face peered from the window of the glowing vehicle as it clattered up Greifswalder Straße, delivering the red cape and its occupant to their midnight rendezvous.

Had it been Weiss on the tram? It must have been, unless the historian had a double in the city, someone who lived out all the excesses that he denied himself. Traditionally, as far as I knew, if you met your doppelgänger one of you had to die, usually the "real" person rather than the other, "inauthentic," self, either that or both of you died. Or else, I couldn't help wondering, had the person in the cape been a mirage?

The next morning, all these questions, each unanswered, were knocking about my head. If it *had* been Weiss, I figured, then it was probably his tube of lipstick, burnt sienna, I'd found in the bathroom that day shortly after starting work. It hadn't occurred to me to check the color on the transvestite's lips but I seemed to remember it was dark, at least not the garish red one might expect from a transvestite although I was far from an expert, with little to refer to aside from the trannies I used to see at clubs in Mexico, with their fake lashes and extravagant names, always startling us with their deep voices that seemed to rise out of a well of hormones.

Thursday, late afternoon. I needed to get out of the house, go for a walk to clear my head. The dreaded migraine had never set in yet the sight of the elderly man in a red cape had thrown me further off course than any throbbing of the temples. At the bathroom mirror I applied a few strokes of makeup, picturing Weiss in front of a mirror in his bedroom, which I had yet to see, doing the same. I found a charcoal pencil I'd once bought at the revamped department store in Alexanderplatz and drew two thick lines, Cleopatra style, below each eye. I dusted my cheeks with soft-color rouge and covered the rest of my face with translucent powder. Mascara usually irritated my eyes but that day something made me reach for the miniature chimney brush to thicken my lashes. Four coats later, each blink weighed down my lids and most of my face had now been brought into sculptural relief, at least as much as the transvestite's, and all that was missing was the mouth. No burnt sienna, just plain red. Yet my red pencil refused to write on my lips. I traced their outline, over and over, following the light dip and the two small crests on either side, but nothing came out. I pressed harder and felt a sharp sting. The pencil must have been doing something. I switched on the mirror's overhead light and discovered that my lips were full of splinters. Each time I pressed them together a sharp pain traveled to the outer edges. The pencil had done more than its job, my mouth a flaming red carnation. I dug out a pair of tweezers from my cosmetics bag and began the extraction.

The phone rang.

"Tatiana?" A voice emerged from the thicket of crackling that always engulfed calls from Mexico.

"Yes?"

"It's Teresa."

"Hello."

"I have a cold so I'm taking a day off from the deli."

"Oh. How is everyone?"

"Fine, everyone is fine. Though Papa wonders why you haven't been in touch these past few months. We haven't received a postcard since July."

Teresa, always the one assigned to fish for information.

"I've been busy. I have a new job."

"I heard. Some kind of professor, right?"

"Historian."

"How are you? Everyone wants to know."

"I'm fine."

"Just fine?"

"Yes . . . What news is there from home?"

"Pickled herring went up ten pesos a kilo."

"What else?"

"Salted beef went up seven pesos."

"Tell me about something else."

"We no longer get our barley from Don Pedro's."

"And what else?"

"Well, we've stepped up challah production, though eggs went up too, so we never run out anymore. And that's includ-ing special orders."

This was no better than my interview with the Simpleton.

"Tell me about people."

"We're all fine . . . But Mama's put on six kilos since you last saw her."

"Oh."

"She wants to know whether you've met someone yet."

The inevitable question.

"Not yet."

"Absolutely no one?"

"No."

"Why not?"

"There's no one to like."

"Maybe you should come back to Mexico."

"That's not the solution."

"Have you really met absolutely no one?"

I hesitated. "No."

"Mama and Papa are going to be very disappointed."

"Aren't seven grandchildren enough?"

"That's not what it's about."

"So what is it about?"

"They want you to be happy."

"How are things with Pablo? Are *you* happy?"

Teresa laughed. "Of course. He's the best husband in the world. And he's so healthy, he never gets sick. Not even headaches."

"That's great. Is anyone else around?"

"What, like right now?"

"Yes."

"No, everyone's at the deli. I'm alone in the house. I told you, it's because I have a cold . . . Tatiana, is everything *really* all right?"

"Yes."

"Are you sure? You'd tell us, right?"

"Of course."

It usually took between five and seven minutes for conversations to reach an impasse. Today it had taken a little over four.

"Okay, then."

"Well, give my love to everyone."

"I will," Teresa answered.

Click. From one second to the next the crackling ended and my lips, which I'd briefly forgotten about, began to sting even more than before the phone had rung. I returned to the bathroom mirror and continued plucking, and as I stood there extracting the splinters from my lips I realized, with great relief, that Teresa hadn't mentioned her children. *What a relief*, was all I could think with each tiny splinter I extracted, *What a relief*. By now each of my siblings had produced at least one kid and most phone calls were about first steps, first words, dietary preferences, sleeping habits, teething updates, and other unsolicited details. It wasn't until I'd hung up the phone and returned to the splinters that I began to wonder whether something had been bothering Teresa, whether there wasn't, just this once, something on her mind apart from her brood. Had someone notified my family of something? Usually there weren't so many questions about my well-being, nor were they ever delivered so insistently. I couldn't help feeling that my sister, following orders from my parents, had been prying. Somewhere, an alarm had been sounded. But who would have contacted them, and why?

The only person who came to mind was Doktor Weiss, who seemed to harbor a few secrets of his own unless I had been hallucinating the night before, which was a possibility, yet the figure in the red cape had seemed so real, I couldn't bring myself to accept it was an illusion. It *was* him, it had to have been him, who else would have the same shock of white hair and thick tangled eyebrows, and if that were indeed the case then my image of him would be radically altered and I would have to start again from zero and conjure up a whole new persona for this historian who, as far as I knew, rarely left home and saw no one but his black dog and hired scribe.

Yet over the days and weeks that followed there were no changes in his behavior, none at all, so I simply kept transcribing, watching my employer out of the corner of my eye as he shuffled through the apartment in his long purple robe that was beginning to open at the seams: this employer of mine who lived with one foot in the past and one in the present, mourning *all that could have been* instead of going out and seeing *all that had become*.

And then one day a letter arrived and once again life turned eventful, although in ways I would have never imagined.

Dear Doktor Weiss,

I hope it is not too much of an imposition to write to you, or an even greater imposition to request the pleasure of a brief meeting at your convenience. Your assistant Tatiana mentioned you were pleased with my answers and it is for this reason that I approach you. I would be delighted to welcome you into my home in Marzahn. Please let me know if you ever have the time or inclination.

With greatest respect,
Jonas Krantz

Doktor Weiss did not decline. He expressed mutual curiosity to meet Jonas Krantz and said he hadn't been to Marzahn in years, or Lichtenberg or Hohenschönhausen for that matter, and it was high time, he said, that he leave the old citadel of Charlottenburg and venture once more into the city's newer limbs. I could tell he viewed the excursion as a welcome adventure, as something pleasingly out of the ordinary, and so I had no choice but to call Jonas and make an appointment. On the phone he was distant but polite. He had just received an urgent commission to code a weather report for transmission over a few international networks, he said, but would of course make time for the historian, and suggested Saturday at five.

On that day, which opened with a fierce winter sun that gave an illusory sense of the changing of seasons, I set out for Charlottenburg to pick Weiss up. On my way to Alexanderplatz I looked out the tram window and to my astonishment there was the Simpleton at her usual post, a little tree swayed by the icy air, in her flowered dress yet no coat, a branch in one hand, shopping bags slung over an arm. Her red scarf was in place, as were her ruddy cheeks and wispy bangs and her plastic open-toed slippers, but there was something missing, her smile. She stood there as she always had but this time did not wear a smile and it was disconcerting to see the Simpleton, no longer a Simpleton, standing there looking so serious. Perhaps after a long duel that had lasted all afternoon the demonic laugh had killed off the smile and from now on this vacant slate that conveyed nothing would be her only expression. What had happened to her since we spoke? I don't think she saw me from where she was standing; as far as I could tell she never looked into the trams passing by, but I turned away just in case.

*   *   *

Weiss opened the door with Murci at his heels and nodded
his customary greeting. "I won't be a moment, take a seat in
the kitchen if you like."

Even with my coat on, the back of the kitchen chair felt
cold, as if there were only a thin layer between my skin and
the wood. The day was chillier than the previous few and I
hadn't dressed warmly enough, and as I rubbed my hands together and blew into them I wondered how the Simpleton
could possibly be standing outside in just a flowered dress.

For the first time in weeks Weiss was not wearing the
long purple robe, and in his grey tweed pants and black turtleneck sweater I could see how very thin he was, the tiny waist,
the concave stomach, the flaccid arms. Now I couldn't imagine that it had been him that night on the tram; the figure I'd
seen had chunky calves, although perhaps the historian had
recently lost weight.

"Cold, are you?" he asked.

"A little."

He paused at the door, evidently searching for a solution,
and all of a sudden his face brightened. "I know just the thing.
Come to my study."

I was finally going to see the room where Weiss spent
most of his hours, the room where he had probably spoken all
those words into the dictaphone, and I eagerly followed him
down the corridor before watching his gnarled hand grip the
doorknob. Unlike the other rooms in the house, the study had

character, I noticed as soon as we stepped in, its own organized clutter and a weather-beaten warmth that enfolded everything. Books rose from the floor in uneven stacks, like primitive chimneys, and the only wall not covered floor to ceiling with shelves boasted a display of painted Italian plates with mythological scenes. The plates hung in two rows of five, like a table set for ten wall climbers. In one corner stood a writing desk with a large blotter and a green lamp. Near the desk Weiss paused at a chest covered by a rather loud folkloric shawl with red, green, blue and yellow stripes, and it was this shawl that he had come for. He pulled it off and handed it to me.

"I bought this in Mexico. One hundred percent wool, or so they told me. It should keep you warm. Just throw it over your shoulders."

The shawl smelled like old wool, a comforting smell despite the cloud of dust that emerged as I "threw" it over my shoulders. Weiss grabbed a cane from a corner of his room, it was the first time I had ever seen him with one, and slipped on a black hat that hid his tangled eyebrows. We were ready to go.

The taxi ride from Charlottenburg to Marzahn took over half an hour. With his hat covering his forehead and eyebrows and the coat collar rising up to his ears with just his eyes and nose escaping, Weiss looked like something out of Gogol as he glued his face to the window, mentally registering the details of every street we passed.

Entering Marzahn by car rather than S-Bahn emphasized the sharp decrease in movement and vibrancy and on that day even the Plattenbaus looked drained of color. The deeper our taxi penetrated the more monotone the architecture grew, the fewer the people on the street. It seemed to be a place with little or no birdsong, as if even the trees were made of concrete, although it was winter, of course, and barrenness was the norm. On our way down Landsberger Allee, formerly known as Lenin Allee, we passed a compound of large brick buildings covered in graffiti, a former slaughterhouse Weiss explained, and to our left, not much farther down the avenue, was the circus Berolina, three red tents encircled by pale yellow trailers, advertising "Europe's best animal trainers," although as Weiss further commented, it would have certainly fallen short of the circuses with which much of Marzahn's Russian community had grown up, especially regarding such things as bears and animal trainers.

"Eighteenth floor? Thank heavens for elevators," he said once we'd found the right Plattenbau and rung Jonas Krantz's buzzer, quickly stepping aside for two gangly teenagers who were exiting the building. Outside the context of his home, Weiss seemed like a snail without its shell, a spineless creature bereft of its armor.

It was obvious Jonas had made an effort—fresh tarts from the bakery, a pretty blue teapot with matching cups and saucers, the sugar jar filled to the brim with brown sugar—and over this little arrangement I kept catching his gaze. I tried to avoid looking at him lest our meeting of eyes should give him the wrong impression, there was *no* unspoken complicity between us, he had to understand, but it was hard, given that he was sitting directly across from me. Once had been enough, it was not to be repeated, I thought to myself as he poured the tea and stirred in the sugar, although I also couldn't help noticing the dark rings under his eyes, especially dark that evening, and how they lent his face an intense aura.

He was excited to meet Weiss, nervous at first, but after the first half hour he relaxed and eased into conversation, quoting bits here and there, throwing out statistics, wearing his intellect on his sleeve. With hesitant strides they spoke about the GDR. Jonas told Doktor Weiss about returning, not long ago, to the house where he had grown up, at Weidenweg 75 in Friedrichshain, and seeing how the building he had so loved, most of the time anyhow, was now a mud-colored mass covered in graffiti with blackened windows and long, gaping holes where the balconies had been torn out. It had deeply saddened him, he said, and he couldn't help wondering why that weary building hadn't been refurbished like all the others on the street.

Weiss told Jonas, in turn, about his visits to the other side of the Wall, and of all the books and candy and postcards from the Pergamon he ended up buying with the East German marks he was forced to exchange each time he crossed over, and of his harrowing experiences with East Berlin doctors, and of the acute inflammation of the liver he came down with on November 9, 1989, so that when everyone else was rushing to the Wall to witness the historic moment, there he was, trapped in a hospital bed in Wedding with abominable food and fuzzy television reception.

They spoke about the merging of East and West Berlin as if they were a pair of human lungs, one pink and healthy and the other tinged with grey like that of a moderate smoker, trying to breathe in unison but every now and then still gasping for air, and although I don't remember who came up with the image in the first place I admit it was one I kept returning to much later, this fusing of two spongy organs, one considerably hardier, breathing in the same elements from the atmosphere and feeding oxygen into the system to keep circulation going at all costs.

At one point I got up to go to the bathroom and while washing my hands I noticed a framed document hanging by the mirror, a list in a childlike scrawl, presumably Jonas's, from when he was younger:

Imagined Etymologies

Brontology: the study of thunder
    Derived from sound traveling up and down the neck of a brontosaurus—emerging from somewhere deep, a rumbling more threatening than its reality

Nephology: the study of clouds
  A mutation of the term neophilia, a liking for new things—change for the sake of change, a desire for novelty
  Or else, nephews of air and water

Anemology: the study of wind
  Derived from anemia, a weak visual presence and atmospheric pallor: on its own wind is invisible, can only be observed through its effects on its surroundings

Ombrology: the study of rain
  Derived from the adjective ombre (shaded or graduated in tone)—rain brings about a certain darkness, casting shadows and wetting the landscape in gradations—like darkness, rain can either activate or extinguish

I was reminded that there was indeed a lot to him, a rich inner landscape as my mother would have said, and upon returning to the living room I stopped trying to avoid his gaze and instead attempted a few smiles but by then his attention was fully given over to my employer.

Dusk fell swiftly, a sheet of gauze thrown over the Plattenbau, and Weiss must have also noted the dramatic change since he abruptly ended the conversation just as Jonas was lifting the teapot to refill everyone's cup.

"Well, it was very nice to meet you," Weiss said, rising from his seat.

"Yes, well, it has been *very* nice," Jonas said, setting the teapot back down. "I have long been an admirer of your work."

The historian nodded, immune to flattery. "Now, where did I leave my cane?"

Jonas's eyes darted around the room before landing on the corner where the cane had been deposited, the same corner, I recalled, into which he had occasionally stared during our interview.

"Let me call you a taxi," he said, and disappeared into another room.

Weiss stood at the center of the room, gazing at the various charts on the walls. "So those are his maps of the sky, are they?"

"I think so."

Jonas returned. "The taxi service isn't answering. Let me walk you over to Landsberger Allee, where we can surely find a cab."

Weiss raised a hand. "No worries. We can find our way. Just tell us where to go."

"I'd rather come with you, if you don't mind."

"We can find our way."

"But if you don't mind . . ." Jonas insisted.

Weiss's grip tightened around the handle of his cane. "I have lived in this city my entire life, with the exception of a few unfortunate years. Don't worry about me."

"Just tell us how to reach the main street," I echoed.

Jonas beckoned us over to the window and pointed to the right. "You see those traffic lights? That's Landsberger Allee. Just stand at the intersection and you should see many taxis. If not, you can go a few streets farther, to the Marzahn Promenade, which doesn't look much like a promenade so make sure you read the signs."

I followed Weiss to the door, amazed, yet again, by how diminished he looked from the back.

At the door Jonas Krantz shot me a longing look.

"Call me," I said.

Outside the Plattenbau there was absolute stillness, as if dusk had waved a wand and vanished all life forms from the playground, park benches and local shop. Weiss suggested cutting through the playground but gave in to my insistence that we keep to the curved path along the buildings since the ground was more level and also, marginally, better lit. We began walking in the direction of Landsberger Allee, or at least in the direction in which Jonas had pointed, though we couldn't be sure, and at the end of the path we took a right and somehow ended up in another communal space surrounded by three unfamiliar Plattenbaus enclosing yet another abandoned playground and shuttered supermarket.

"Now what?" Weiss asked, unease rather than anger in his voice.

I was about to propose retracing our steps and returning to Jonas's building when they closed in on us, like two strong gales blowing from either direction, and even under the weak light cast from the entrances we could make out their pink faces and upturned noses; in the twilight area between the Plattenbaus where Weiss and I had lost our way, the historian insisting we go one direction and I the other, the two men appeared out of nowhere.

As far as I could tell there were only two of them but it might as well have been an entire gang. The fat one had eyes like two tiny buttons jammed into a mass of dough and a re-pulsively thick neck like the neck of a steer, as if ten wooden yokes could not hold him back, and then there was his friend, his face partially hidden under a hood so that all I could see was a thin gash of a mouth and the snub nose, and in the desert of the Plattenbaus this pair bled forth like a dark stain on the unalloyed monotony.

Weiss gasped. I had never heard him make a sound like that before, and when I heard him gasp I realized the gravity of our situation, for here we were, the old man with his sol-emn hat and cane and the Mexican in her folkloric shawl like a bird of paradise, removed from all familiar contexts and safety nets. The steer with the thick neck snorted at Doktor Weiss, who muttered something under his breath, I'm not sure what he said but it seemed to inflame them, and before I knew it the steer, with one small shove, had knocked the old man down like a playing card. Weiss's reflexes were quick and he tried to stop his fall with his cane but the cane wasn't angled correctly and it fell with a loud clatter, almost at the same time as the historian himself, whose body hit the ground with a thump.

I leaped forward to help Weiss and fetch the hat that came rolling off his head but the ghoul in the hood grabbed me by the neck, forced me into a headlock and clamped his free hand on my crotch. From somewhere on the ground Weiss moaned but I couldn't turn to see what was happening, although out of the corner of my eye I saw the steer run to snatch up Weiss's hat and begin tossing it in the air, higher and higher, his booming laughter bouncing off the concrete walls of the Plattenbaus.

Sometimes, in the past, while watching horror movies I had wondered how I would react in a desperate situation, whether I would scream out for help or whether my tongue would freeze in fear, and that evening it was definitely the latter. I simply couldn't produce a sound, my vocal chords seemed paralyzed and my whole body limp and ineffective, unable to even protest when the burly steer yanked the woolen shawl off my back and ripped it to shreds.

I heard something crack; I didn't know whether it was a bone in Weiss's body or the wood of his cane, but something cracked in two, or perhaps in three or four, who knows. My head was still caught in a headlock, the big hand still jammed in my crotch, not really moving, just menacingly wedged there. I heard the sound of a bottle being smashed against the pavement and the historian moaning again but the guy with the hood didn't loosen his grip for a second.

For all its horror our encounter with the thugs did not last long, but that was only because of the fog, the fog that all of a sudden descended over everything, tumbling down in a wispy sea. A tentative veil at first, it soon thickened and branched out in one hundred directions, its open arms of moisture spreading to embrace everything within reach. It was as if the clouds, filled with curiosity, had come down to examine our sphere, and from one moment to the next all I could see was the ghost of the thug who clasped me, an indistinct mass whose features were melting into the whiteness around us. Everything was being effaced at incredible speed. For it was indeed the clouds, the clouds that had lowered themselves to ground level, coming to our rescue when all seemed lost, when it truly seemed as if Weiss and I would never leave Marzahn alive, two crushed fireflies left to sputter out on the pavement.

I felt the grip around my neck loosening. Confused by the sudden change in the atmosphere, the thugs grunted in monosyllables, their voices echoing eerily in the mist.

"Alex?"

"What?"

"Can you . . ."

"What?"

". . . See me?"

"No."

"What?"

"No."

"I can't either."

"What the fuck?"

"The old Jew probably laid a curse on us."

The other met these words with silence, as if seriously contemplating the possibility of an ancient Hebrew curse.

The arm around my neck withdrew. Seconds later, the hand in my crotch released its hold. I was dropped, jettisoned, pushed away, thrown to the ground like a discarded whore. Through the fog I heard an anxious exchange of voices, perhaps a plan of action being discussed, and felt a bustling around me followed by the eventual, and needless to say heavenly, reverberations of boots retreating. It sounded like the two men were heading in different directions, one to the right and one to the left, though I had no way of knowing and all that mattered was that with every passing minute their steps grew fainter. Once they seemed a long way off I sat up and rubbed my neck, realizing as I tried to inspect my body that it was indeed impossible to see anything, anything at all.

"Doktor Weiss?" I called out.

There was no response, not even a muffled SOS, only the silence of a stilled city.

"Doktor Weiss?"

I wasn't certain, but from somewhere a few feet away I thought I heard a moan. I walked tentatively in its direction.

"Doktor Weiss?" I said again.

No, it wasn't a moan.

The only thing I could do was to find my way back to a familiar part of the city and get help for the elderly historian. This fog was no doubt unusual, something entirely beyond normal meteorological activity, and as I tried to find my way I sensed it had spread far beyond the interstices between the Marzahn Plattenbaus, for there was no end of it in sight.

Now that everything seemed to be in *extremis* I found the main street without any trouble, or at least I found what I assumed was Landsberger Allee, though there was, of course, no way to be sure, and so I began groping my way along, listening to the cries of anguished individuals who all of a sudden found themselves shipwrecked two doors from home. I took small steps, scared of tripping or of trampling something, hugging traffic lights and streetlamps as if they were buoys, the iron cold and clammy to the touch. The bulbs were lit and for once I was delighted to see their orangey glow though the light was diffuse and barely shone through the curtain of fog, yet the glow, warm and hazy, was just bright enough to help me find my way from one lamp to the next, like a small boat following a procession of flares at sea.

A thick smell hung in the air, a smell that spoke of dungeon, as if one thousand Victorian chimneys had been tipped over and the lethal combination of coal fires and urban vapor had been decanted into the vast cavities of Berlin, crawling up walls and skimming the surface of the Spree, coating the shell of the S-Bahn and halting trains midjourney. Yes, it was like those Victorian pea soupers I remember reading about in

English novels, although thankfully without the carbon dioxide thrown in, and surely whiter and more translucent and purer than the mixtures of yore, since our fog, far more celestial, had fewer man-made contaminants.

I had no idea which way to walk since the fog had claimed each landmark and there was nothing to navigate by. I searched the sky for my beloved television tower but it was nowhere to be found, not a single glint of metal or hint of soaring cement. It was hard to tell how high the fog rose, perhaps some fifty to one hundred meters, and the density seemed to vary from area to area. On some streets the fog was thicker and visibility nil, on others I could see the vague outline of my hand when I held it right up to my eyes.

On what must have been a corner since the sidewalk fell away I brushed against what felt like a warm woolen sleeve, obviously another human being. The person let out a startled cry and moved away before I had time to discover whether it was a man or a woman, as if I were some kind of revenant when in reality I was just as startled. This was the closest I had ever come to experiencing blindness, apart from the time in the bowling alley. At another point I felt some-one graze my hand, almost caressing my wrist, but again I could not attach a face, or any feature for that matter, to the individual, so it was nothing more than a disembodied caress, seconds of intimacy with a stranger. We were all ghosts, specters, wraiths, it was impossible to tell who or what had substance, who or what was an illusion.

For the entire duration of the fog I did not hear a single car engine; every vehicle in the city, I thought, had probably come to a standstill, stalled in the miasma, blinded like the rest of us. So I crossed streets without thinking twice, although unsure at times where one ended and the next began.

Halfway into town, or what I sensed was halfway, I heard the voice of an old man, not Weiss's, of course, but someone else's, crying out for help, explaining that he had to get home urgently to take his medicine, four grams of Rivotril before eight o'clock, but of course no one could help him and his cries of "*Bitte, bitte*" were ignored; how could anyone have possibly done anything? In this fog there were no heroes.

I'd just taken a bite of cloud, detecting a hint of fuel or sulfur as if an airplane had flown through, when I caught sight of the topmost tip of the television tower, my beacon rising like a grand spire. The fog was indeed dissipating, just a little, in patches, and as I walked in the direction of Alexanderplatz I began to note familiar markers being restored: a yellow mailbox, a particular tree, the S-Bahn tracks, corners of the big department store, floors eighteen to twenty of a Plattenbau, tiny lagoons of existence as the city gradually reclaimed her face.

By the time I reached the surprisingly calm police station on Immanuelkirchstraße a pervasive dampness had seeped into my clothes, even into my underpants and brassiere, and I shivered as I awaited my turn inside, although there was no one else waiting. After two cups of milky coffee from the vending machine I told the police officer—no, I insisted—that he send a car to Marzahn, and fast. In dramatic detail I described Weiss's fragile constitution, resurrecting my image of a snail without a shell, and expressed my fear that the thugs might return now that the fog was lifting. The officer seemed a bit confused about the fog, and was far more interested, it seemed, in the identity of "this Jonas Krantz," and it was only when he asked me for the exact time we left Jonas's apartment that I glanced at my wrist and discovered my watch was missing. That caress in the fog, the one encounter that had seemed somewhat tender and intimate, had actually been an act of deceit. But I wasn't worried about my forty-euro Swatch, I was worried about Doktor Weiss, and I did not rest until I saw the police officer pick up the phone and dispatch a car.

A dazzling sun spread over the morning. Due to the overwhelming humidity of the previous evening the streets were carpeted with posters and advertisements that had peeled off thousands of pillars and kiosks. I bought two local papers, ones I'd never noticed before, and leafed through them over breakfast, amazed at how swiftly the journalists had measured the effects of the fog. "Berlin in New Crisis of Erasure," read one headline, drawing obvious parallels between the city's past and this bizarre meteorological phenomenon. More interestingly, the papers described the anarchy that the fog had unleashed: across Berlin locks had unfastened and the ink on contracts and other documents dissolved; on every street doors had swung open and closed, each hinge becoming an autonomous entity left to operate on its own. It had been a real abracadabra moment, they wrote, in which rules were put on hold and the laws of physics suspended, as all and everything succumbed to this sweeping act of condensation.

A record number of crimes had been committed, highly unusual for a city that boasted such a low crime rate: the clouds had provided a moment of transcendence at ground level but also opened up a small window for depravity. Rapes, muggings, unprecedented violence. A Turkish teenager was stabbed to death in Neukölln. Two further deaths were reported, of people falling into the Spree (the railing was too low); curiously, both casualties were Russian although one a resident of Marzahn and the other a tourist from Vladivostok.

Everywhere, the reporters added, doors had unlocked on their own, leading to the following statistics: thirty-eight inmates had escaped from the prison in Moabit, fifty-four from the state asylum, six from a small clinic on the shores of Berlin, twelve hospital patients in pale blue robes, fed up with the nurses and insisting they were healthy, had bolted, and, finally, a few elderly people from an old folks' home—though they hadn't gotten far—were found wandering, slipperless, in the vicinity.

The fog, meanwhile, had offered a splendid opportunity for thieves, who grabbed whatever was in front of them, pulling at every bag in reach without knowing whether it was a lady's purse or a student's backpack or a tramp's life's possessions. Most shops had closed for fear of robbers, except for the KaDeWe, which had stubbornly remained open and the next day reported many items missing from its inventory, mostly from counters near the main entrance (gloves, cosmetics, perfume, umbrellas). According to the saleswomen, the fog rode up the escalators and spread through each floor, impregnating the clothes and cracking the wooden hangers, while at the Staatsbibliothek the head librarian had the presence of mind to seal off the bookshelves with plastic sheets and had issued an urgent call to librarians across the city to follow suit. Museum guards and curators ran to take similar measures and fortunately most of the art in the city was saved, except for a few conceptual art installations at galleries in Mitte, which didn't matter since they could easily be replicated.

There were countless reports of people walking into walls and scraping their foreheads or noses, and of others knocking each other down in the street. Some were bitten by dogs on whose tails they had unwittingly tread, especially in neighborhoods like Friedrichshain where the number of dogs lying outside cafes often equaled the number of customers at the tables.

It had been an eventful day for the whores on Oranienburger Straße as well. With their breath-defying corsets and thigh-high white boots they received a lot of attention although they didn't necessarily make much of a profit since most of the customers vanished without paying. The whores were groped by men from all walks of life, and especially by those who normally wouldn't have had the nerve to approach them but who, now, anxious to make the most of this mantle of concealment, had grabbed at everything female with satyr-like frenzy. Women outside the trade also had their breasts and behinds fondled by passing strangers, and some, apparently, later dreamed of being reunited with their fondlers.

All in all, it had been an exceptional day.

I wasn't sure what to bring, I couldn't imagine he liked cut flowers, so I found two books of poetry, Georg Trakl and Zbigniew Herbert, and a box of pralines; incongruous hospital gifts perhaps, but I couldn't think of anything else.

There he lay, without his carapace, or rather encased in another kind of carapace, this one hard and white and heavy. The cast covered a large part of his body, at least half I would say, although it was hard to tell since most of him lay beneath a polyester blanket. Two broken ribs and an arm with multiple fractures, plus serious internal bleeding, was what the doctor had said over the phone. He was lucky it hadn't been worse.

I thought he was asleep, his eyes shut and his eyebrows quiescent, but as soon as I drew up my chair his lids sprang open.

"Is that you?" His voice had dimmed, the frontal shock of hair hung limply.

"Yes, Doktor Weiss."

"What took you so long?"

"I wasn't allowed to visit you in intensive care."

Weiss's room was directly in front of the elevators and from where I sat I could hear the constant opening and closing of doors as well as a loud, exasperating beep each time there was a stop at his floor.

"How long was I there?"

"Four days."

"And what day is it today?"

"Friday."

"That means nothing to me."

Weiss leaned into a stack of pillows as if the weight of his entire past were accumulated in his lower back. He studied me for a minute and then turned towards the window, beyond which yawned a bubblegum-pink billboard touting a mobile phone company. "I've had many dreams these past few days, dream after dream after dream. I don't know how my brain was able to sift through so many images."

"What were they about?"

He ignored my question. "Tell me, how many were there that day in Marzahn? Four, six, eight?"

"I think there were two."

"Only two?"

"Yes."

"And did Jonas come to save us?"

"No, the clouds did."

A nurse walked in and took his temperature, which was down to normal. They discussed dinner. No peppers or carrots, he requested, and eggs only if they were well cooked. The nurse nodded to everything he said, rearranged the pillows behind his head, and left the room.

"The clouds . . . Which clouds?"

"The clouds that came down to save us."

He gazed at me wordlessly yet I recognized the expression of polite quizzicality. I didn't feel like explaining. It was a good moment to bring out my presents. He already had the Trakl, an older edition, of course, but said he would read the Herbert. As for the pralines, he would try one later though he was meant to stay away from sweets.

"So you are leaving Berlin," he said, once the books and unopened box of chocolates had been examined and placed on the night table.

"Yes."

"We'll miss you, Murci and I, but understand your decision."

"It was leading up to this for a while. It's not only because of what happened last Saturday."

"Of course not. It's never about just one event, but rather a whole sequence of much smaller events, all those loaded seconds and minutes and hours that lead toward a decisive moment. . . . Jonas is looking after Murci, is he?"

"Yes. He's been taking him for walks and says he's doing fine."

"Do you already have your ticket?"

"My parents booked it from Mexico."

Neither of us said anything for a while. Weiss glanced out the window a few more times and reread the Trakl book jacket. I studied him when he wasn't looking, amazed, once

more, by this elderly snail without a shell, this decrepit historian bereft of his universe, hooked up to a drip in a hospital
bed, wearing an insipid blue gown instead of his rich purple
robe. The gaps in conversation were not because there was
nothing to say but rather because there was *too much* to say
and I simply didn't know where to begin, and during each gap
I heard the opening and closing of the elevator doors as more
unfortunate patients were wheeled in or new visitors arrived
with chocolates and flowers. There was so much I still wanted
to know about Doktor Weiss and so much I felt he didn't yet
know about me, so many things about myself I wanted to set
straight and so many doubts I still had regarding his life. In
fact, I felt he didn't know me at all and now there would never
be time to tell him. He would never know, for instance, about
my aversion to artificial light or my experiences with Jonas
Krantz and other young Berliners, or how I dreaded Sundays
yet insisted on spending them alone and how with each Sunday sun arose the question of how I was going to fill the hours,
and all those other little patterns in my life that repeated themselves ad nauseam but had, admittedly, loosened a little, ta-
pered in importance, thanks to my job as transcriber. And aside
from all the things I wanted to tell him about my life I still
had one burning question which I held back each time I was
on the verge of articulating it. Finally, though, when the historian began to close his eyes with greater frequency and I
sensed our session was coming to an end, I took a deep breath
and seized the next lapse in conversation to throw it out.

"Doktor Weiss," I began, trying to sound as deferential as possible, "I was just wondering . . . I hope this doesn't sound peculiar, but do you by any chance own a red cape? And were you traveling one night at around midnight on a tram from Alexanderplatz in a black skirt and this red cape?"

He looked at me and closed his eyes.

"I'm sorry, maybe I shouldn't be asking," I said, half withdrawing my question yet hoping, dearly, for a response.

"I'm tired, it's time for my nap," he said with his eyes still closed, "but will I see you again before you leave?"

"My flight is in four days."

"Then come again to say good-bye, will you? I would very much like that. We can then continue our conversation," he said, promising me nothing. He raised his left arm, the one without a cast, a few inches from the bed. I quickly leaned over and grabbed his hand, assuming that that was his wish. He squeezed my hand in a tired, limp grip, then let it fall, a puppet cut free from its string.

If only I could interview Murci, I couldn't help thinking as I waited outside for the elevator, if only I could ask that totemic animal whether it *had* been Weiss on the tram and if so, what exactly he had been doing and how he spent his days when he wasn't speaking into the dictaphone, and also what had happened down in the Gestapo bowling alley that night, whether I had indeed entered the German Hades or just a small, displaced corner of Mictlan, for I couldn't help feeling that this dog held the answer to many questions and that it was only a matter of prying open his tiny jaws and extracting them from his mouth.

If only I could interview Murci, I thought yet again upon arriving at the hospital a few days later to be told that Weiss had developed an infection and was once more in intensive care, although this time the doctor wasn't *too* worried, only cautious, but cautious enough to refuse me entry even when I told him it was my last day in Berlin and that I couldn't leave without saying good-bye to my employer. But no, he was unbudgeable, my pleas did not move him, and I would not be granted entry, it was far too great a risk, he said, tapping his pen on his clipboard and making a sound as impertinent as the words he was speaking, too great a risk, he repeated, especially with young people, who expose themselves to all kinds of bacteria and one could never be sure what they were carrying.

And so it was that I never saw Weiss again, although in a way our last exchange had indeed been a good-bye and I couldn't really have hoped for much more, and furthermore, I wasn't sure how much should be said about the incident in Marzahn, or whether I need tell him about the four hours I'd spent with the *Kriminalpolizei* wading through their database, inspecting hundreds of mug shots of young delinquents and fascist hoodlums, although *there was no guarantee*, the police reminded me, that these thugs were definitely fascist, they said, *No guarantee that they even had fascist inclinations*. I also need not tell Weiss about the piercing headache I developed by the

time I'd finished with the *Kriminalpolizei*, and how for days af-
terwards I was kept awake by the faces I'd seen, and how my
heart nearly leaped out of my chest the night some drunkard
rang my bell at 4:25 in the morning and though deep down I
knew it was only a random drunkard on a Saturday night I
couldn't help fearing that our attackers had jumped on the
S-Bahn and come to Prenzlauer Berg just to get one final thrill
out of the Mexican with the warm crotch, though, of course,
they would have no way of knowing where I lived. I also never
got to tell Weiss about the *Kriminalpolizei* themselves, how one
of them looked like an overgrown schoolboy with a dopey face
and how the other was a handsome blond with green eyes who
chewed his gum loudly between questions and made fun of his
"new colleague," the overgrown schoolboy, who still didn't
know his way around the building and kept taking the wrong
turn. I never told Weiss any of this, although he would also,
no doubt, be summoned to the police station.

After all, who wanted to discuss the incident, of seeing
your little world and all it stands for fall apart in seconds,
watching as a disease is injected into your body where it will
begin to fester no matter how much you try to fight it with
the force of reason, of feeling your sense of equilibrium in the
city destroyed from one moment to the next; who needed to
discuss all of this?

In the end we were lucky, Doktor Weiss and I, unlike
our ninety-four-year-old florist in Mexico, whom I suddenly

thought of, mugged one Sunday morning at the wholesale market where he'd gone at six a.m. to buy flowers, and who died from injuries to the head, a man with eighteen grandchildren and a bundle of dignity, knocked down for a few pesos. At least Weiss had lived through the beating, or whatever it was the thick-necked steer had done to him, for we would never quite know, but the important thing was, surely, that the doctors managed to stop the internal bleeding and as for a few broken bones, well at that age they were no small thing, but it seemed he would emerge intact from that too, and even with the new infection he had caught there was Jonas, who pledged to look after him once the historian returned home.

Once you decide to leave, you view a city through an entirely different lens. The simplest of actions, actions you have repeated one hundred, maybe a thousand, times, swell in significance since each time may now be the last: the last time you buy bread at the bakery, the last time you ride on the U-Bahn Line 2, the last time you get your boots fixed at the cobbler, the last time you go to the newsagent's for a travel pass or a pack of gum. There were so many things I would miss, I realized, even things I hadn't seen in a while, like the stone-faced museum guards from the days when I still went to museums and the scenester kids plowing through the flea markets in search of the holy vintage grail and the stern women from the bank and the post office with their eighties hairdos and the ice-cream place on Stargarder Straße, where there was always a line, even in winter, and that German punctuality, which made you miss your bus by seven seconds but also ensured you arrived at your appointments on time, and of course the voice of the S-Bahn announcer as he rolled off the stations and Alexanderplatz with its ever-changing face and the yellow streetcars, napping or in motion.

In a similar way, streets acquired a new sheen, as if I were discovering them for the first time, especially my own street, where I began noticing many details I'd failed to notice before, like the way the crests of the two trees on the corner seemed to interlock, and the graffiti on the streetlamp with the broken bulb, and the blue curtains with embroidered yellow stars hanging in the second floor window of the house three doors down. The apartment had been my home for only half a year but now that I was leaving it came to embody every Berlin home I'd ever had, each its own repository of reverie and melancholy and downtrodden expectation, a little cave of solitude I'd both shunned and withdrawn to depending on mood.

But in the midst of all this I felt like the city had given up on me, that the moment I handed in my notice and had my ticket to Mexico, Berlin turned its back on a former inhabitant. Even the people with whom I crossed paths on the street seemed to harden in attitude as if no longer heeding the impulse to be civil since soon I would be gone, or else they were extra aggressive in reproach for my having decided to leave when they were staying put and sticking it out, and I almost felt like grabbing the impatient bus conductor by the shoulders and saying, Look, I'm not from here and as it is I have given five years of my life to this country and am now ready to return to my own, with its own cauldron of problems.

I also found I had more patience for some things, now that I knew I would soon never have to deal with them again, and yet less patience for others. I could finally stop making an effort and actually let myself act out the irritation I had smothered all this time, so when a jogger seized the last supermarket cart I snapped at her, and when my upstairs neighbor, Felix the accountant, played the Scorpions at four in the morning I didn't think twice about going up to complain and even looked over his shoulder at the dark outline on the wall, which for some inexplicable reason he had yet to cover up. All the shyness and inhibition I'd felt during my years in Berlin fell away and in the last weeks and days my spoken German flowed more smoothly than ever as I found myself being assertive in a way I'd never dared to before, a final battle cry before heading back to the New World.

At moments I felt a huge wave of relief, and at others a pang of incipient nostalgia, knowing that soon all this would belong firmly and squarely to the past, to a phase in my life, "the Berlin years" perhaps, and that once I reached Mexico and succeeded in resuscitating my life there I would probably feel a reluctance to return for realistically, the only way to move on is to avoid sentimentality about the past, especially the recent past, which will always try to reclaim you.

I saw Jonas Krantz a sixth and final time, at the airport. On this occasion I was pleased to see him and even kissed him on the lips, aware that there was little danger of things intensifying once I boarded the plane. There was still time for a quick coffee once I'd checked in my two suitcases and box of books, so we found a café and sat down. Jonas promised to continue looking after Murci until Doktor Weiss was released from the hospital. I promised to write to him from Mexico. He promised to get my deposit back from the landlords and see to it that they didn't charge me for holes in the wall or cracks in the floorboards or stale air or all the other things they would probably search for. I left him the sound machine to see if it would help with his insomnia. And, finally, we spoke of the inevitable subject we'd already discussed over and over on the phone, Jonas claiming he hadn't seen the fog or even heard about it later, while I insisted, again and again, on the existence of this tremendous gesture of nature that had taken over the city. And then we spoke about the incident before the fog, Jonas reminding me how it could have been prevented had we only allowed him to walk us to the taxi stand or if we had simply waited half an hour for a taxi, though we both knew there was no point in dwelling on it.

"Well, as they used to say, *Mücke die einen Löwen gestochen hat, fängt sich in einer Spinnwebe.*"

"What do you mean?"

"'The mosquito that stings the lion gets trapped in the spider's web.' I heard from my neighbors this morning that the guys who attacked you were later beaten up by a group of punks from Friedrichshain. It was quite a brawl, supposedly, and one of them is in the hospital in a coma."

At the gate we kissed again, one last compression of the lips before parting ways forever, and I had a vague, but only vague, flashback to my departure from Mexico five years ago, to the limp hugs of my siblings and the teary hugs of my mother, thinking of how within less than twenty-four hours we would be replaying that very scene but in reverse, with my siblings surely ruing my return and my mother thrilled to have me back, though perhaps no one really cared anymore and I wouldn't receive any reception, or only a small one, and how before I knew it, within a week or two, I would have fallen right back into the triangular configuration of home-deli-salon, though now that my siblings had flown the nest my mother promised me my own room, my brothers' former room since it was larger, as well as unlimited use of the car if I ever learned how to drive.

The seat next to mine was free, which was just as well since no one would distract me from my thoughts as the plane roared down the runway, lifted into the air and climbed higher and higher, the distance swiftly growing between me and this somber city that I had loved and hated in equal measure or, better said, I had never known *what* I felt. Down below, just as the plane tilted to the right, I caught sight of the metal sphere of the television tower glinting in the sun, asserting its dominion over the beautiful East, and unless my eyes were fooling me I could see, just barely, a bright figure across the street from Alexanderplatz, a speck of color right by the Deutsche Bank cash machines, though it might have just been a flag or a post or some other vertical object worthy of attention, a new urban fixture that would now be lost to me, as would so many other sights offered from the windows of the tram and the S-Bahn, but I certainly couldn't start thinking about them now.

Before reaching cruising altitude the plane sliced through a thick layer of cloud and for a few seconds there was nothing but white outside the window and I couldn't help feeling, as we cut through the ephemeral landscape slowly thinning and dispersing and branching out in a thousand unmappable directions, that this moment had been prepared especially for me, some kind of aerial requiem held in honor of the city I was leaving behind, and in the end, I remember thinking a few minutes later as the Lufthansa stewardess rattled down the aisle with her drinks cart, there was little difference between clouds and shadows and other phenomena given shape by the human imagination.

ACKNOWLEDGMENTS

I would like to thank my splendid agent, Anna Stein, as well as my fairy godmother, Irene Skolnick. And of course my wise and wonderful editor, Lauren Wein, whose dedication saw this book into print. I am also indebted to those very dear friends around the world whose inspiring feedback and/or faith over the years were invaluable. You know who you are. Lastly, I want to give thanks to my family: to my parents, Betty and Homero, and my sister, Eva, my astral twin.